D0821584

In Plain Arabic

In Plain Arabic

A Play in Two Acts

Lenin El-Ramly

Translated by Esmat Allouba

The American University in Cairo Press

Arabic text copyright © 1992 by Lenin El-Ramly

Translation copyright © 1994 by
The American University in Cairo Press
113 Sharia Kasr el Aini
Cairo, Egypt

First published in Arabic in 1992 as *bi-l-'Arabi al-fasih*
Protected under the Berne Convention

Dar el Kutub No. 3259/94
ISBN 977 424 342 0

Printed in Egypt at the Printshop of the American University in Cairo
Library of Congress Cataloging-in-Publication Data

Ramli, Linin.
    In plain Arabic : a play in two acts / by Lenin El-Ramly ;
    translated by Esmat Allouba. — [Cairo] : American
    University in Cairo Press, 1994.
            p. ;   cm.
                                                    94-961130

I dedicate this translation to my niece, Naela Farouky, who skillfully reenacted most of the play for me during the initial translation process.

— Esmat Allouba

Contents

Translator's Preface

What made me decide to translate *In Plain Arabic?* I have been living abroad for many years, and this play was a new door to a world I have always tried to keep my roots in. The fact that its performance was permitted in Egypt and that it was honored by Kuwait made me sigh with relief in the realization that culture in the Arab world had finally found its voice—a feeling that was also the main theme of reviews in the Arab and non-Arab press. I have to admit that I was amazed to learn about the play through the English press before the Egyptian papers, and I wanted the people who had read those English reviews to be able to read the play.

But of course there was the major problem of preserving the diversity of Arabic dialects while writing in English. The only solution was to try to magnify the typical national traits of different characters through the choice of vocabulary, for instance by making some typically American and others typically British. Inevitably, this does not come close to Lenin El-Ramly's skillful portrayal of his characters. Nevertheless I hope this translation will give pleasure to those who did not have the opportunity to see the play on stage and who would otherwise miss a daring political and cultural message by an artful Egyptian writer.

Author's Introduction

Some people believe that with this play I have rashly criticized the Arabs, thus attracting the governmental and popular wrath of Arabs of all nationalities. Others think that I will suffer the anger of Egyptians, as I have been unfair to Mustafa, the Egyptian character in the play, by equating him with the rest of the Arabs. And, most serious of all, there are those who fear that I will not be safe from the annoyance of the Egyptian government and authorities.

While some worry that the play could be accused of falling into the trap of propaganda for the Palestinian cause at a time when that cause is finished, others insist on the contrary that I have made myself a target because I have taken the side of the West against the Arab East to which I belong.

Some have smiled (out of pity or spite?) and said that I have stepped on a hornets' nest, because the play will aggravate not just one party but all parties, without exception. Yet I cannot deny that I have been congratulated for—I am told—writing a skillfully balanced play that satisfies all sides (with the exception of an allusion here and there that I was advised to omit).

But in fact the problem during the long months in which I struggled to write this play was not the desire to avoid offending anyone, the dilemma was with myself. I believe that the basic problem I face, in common with any writer, is in guiding myself to the truth of what I really wish to express—from the depth of my soul, not the tip of my tongue. I have specific opinions, tendencies, and principles, but when I sit down to write—assuming I am honest with myself—I will discover that these opinions, tendencies, and principles I embrace are good only for newspaper articles, radio or television interviews, or coffeeshop chatter: they will never be enough to write a play.

So my pen hesitates over every detail no matter how small: every line of dialogue, character or place name, description of a scene, stage prop, pause in the action, entry or exit of a character, and so on. And every time, I ask myself tens of questions about this or that, striving for meaning and accuracy.

The answers do not always come immediately. It may take days or months, and there are those questions to which I find an answer only after the completion of the play, or even after its performance. Sometimes then I discover what it was I wanted to say, and sometimes the discovery has to be left to later works!

The play has been accused of pessimism and a cruelty that borders on self-flagellation. I hope I am mistaken and that the situation of the Arabs is better than its reflection in this play.

It has been said that writing is a fictional means of containing terror: I implore my readers and audience to sympathize with my terror.

Cast

THE TELEVISION CREW

FEMALE ANNOUNCER (Sadiqa Salih, Egyptian)
MALE ANNOUNCER (Amin Falih, Egyptian)
DIRECTOR (MALE: Ukasha, Egyptian)
CAMERAMAN (Lutfi, Egyptian)

THE STUDENTS

Women

AMAL (Palestinian)   HIKMAT (Egyptian)
          RABHA (Gulf)

Men

ADHAM (Jordanian)   MIGHWAR (Moroccan)
ANTAR (Iraqi)   MUSTAFA (Egyptian)
FAYEZ (Palestinian)   SAKHR (Syrian)
LAYTH (Libyan)   SAYF (Saudi)
JASIR (Algerian)   SIMAAN (Lebanese)
KHUZAA (Gulf)   SU'DUD (Sudanese)
LUQMAN (Lebanese)   TAMMAM (Tunisian)
          YAZID (Yemeni)

OTHERS

EVE (English)   PROFESSOR WISDOM (English)
FIVE EUROPEAN STUDENTS   SUPERVISOR in disco (English)
GEORGE (English: hotelier)   THREE ROBBERS (English)
GIRL with umbrella (English)   TWO ARAB MEN, their WIVES,
MARGARET (English)   and RETINUE
INSPECTOR (English)   YOUNG ENGLISHMAN

Act One

PROLOGUE

Dimmed lighting. Start of a musical phrase. The title "In Plain Arabic" on the backdrop projection screen. At one side of the stage sits a television DIRECTOR *in front of a controls unit with a* CAMERAMAN. *A* MALE *and a* FEMALE ANNOUNCER *are under adjacent spotlights.*

FEMALE ANNOUNCER: Ladies and Gentlemen . . .

MALE ANNOUNCER: Welcome to your truthful program . . .

F. ANNOUNCER: "In Plain Arabic" . . .

M. ANNOUNCER: Prepared and presented by . . .

F. ANNOUNCER: Sadiqa Salih . . .

M. ANNOUNCER: And Amin Falih . . .

F. ANNOUNCER: Conveyed to you by Arabsat Satellite . . .

M. ANNOUNCER: The satellite channel . . .

F. ANNOUNCER: For the whole Arab world.

[*A dramatic musical phrase, the program signature tune.*]

F. ANNOUNCER: Dear viewers . . .

M. ANNOUNCER: Please excuse this interruption, but we have to make the following statement.

F. ANNOUNCER: The program we are presenting to you tonight . . .

M. ANNOUNCER: Has a story behind it.

F. ANNOUNCER: We set out with intentions of honesty, truth, and accuracy . . .

M. ANNOUNCER: But after filming a portion of the program . . .

F. ANNOUNCER: We realized that the recorded picture did not reflect the whole truth.

M. ANNOUNCER: Therefore we have decided to show you, for the first time . . .

F. ANNOUNCER: What happens behind the cameras.

M. ANNOUNCER: Including us and the director and the cameraman.

F. ANNOUNCER: The show is not for adults only.

M. ANNOUNCER: Nor is it a threat to the weak of heart.

F. ANNOUNCER: But we advise you, before watching it . . .

M. ANNOUNCER: To first ask yourselves: Do you really want us to present you with the whole truth?

F. ANNOUNCER: Or would a quarter of the truth suffice?

M. ANNOUNCER: Do you want it pure and unadulterated?

F. ANNOUNCER: Or would you rather have it frilly?

M. ANNOUNCER: Would you require the truth and nothing but the truth?

F. ANNOUNCER: Or would you prefer . . . its closest relative?

M. ANNOUNCER: Would you let us face you with the truth, without flying into a rage . . .

F. ANNOUNCER: Whoever you are . . .

M. ANNOUNCER: And regardless of your patriotic affiliations and beliefs?

F. ANNOUNCER: Naturally, you would all reply Yes! Yes!

M. ANNOUNCER: So be it . . . . But remember, very clearly . . .

BOTH: You asked for it!

[*Lights out.*]

DIRECTOR'S VOICE: Silence everyone! . . . Stand by. Three, two, one, *action!*

[*Gradual lighting. Scene: Hyde Park in London. A group of Arab* STUDENTS *approach the audience.*]

ALL: We are Arab students who live in London.

SOMEONE: No. . . . No. . . . Wrong. . . . "Living in London."

ALL [*moving closer to the audience*]:
We are Arab students . . . living in London. We are sending this to our beloved parents . . . everywhere . . . in the great Arab world. . . .

MUSTAFA: In Egypt, the guarded and protected land.

ADHAM: In the Jordan Valley.

SAKHR: In the throbbing heart of the Arab World . . . Syria.

LUQMAN: In the Paris of the East . . . Lebanon.

SU'DUD [*Sudanese accent, loose and drunk throughout the play*]: Also Sudan.

ANTAR: And Iraq, the great gatekeeper of the East.

LAYTH: And the great Socialist People's Libyan Arab Jamahiriya.

TAMMAM: And green Tunisia.

MIGHWAR: And white Morocco.

KHUZAA: And the valiant Gulf states.

SAYF: And the holy land of the Hijaz.

JASIR: And Algeria, the land of a million martyrs.

YAZID: And happy Yemen.

FAYEZ: And Palestine . . . land of the Arab awakening.

[*They move into formations accompanied by the anthem "My Beloved Homeland."*]

ALL: Our honorable parents. . . . Love to you all.
Rest assured, we are all fine.
Everything is all right.
All we miss is seeing you.
We are all brothers and brethren here;
Meeting in a foreign land, united for better or for worse,
Resisting the debauchery of the West with full will and determination.
We are addicted to acquiring knowledge, as if knowledge were a drug!
So that we can come home and pour our knowledge on our beloved land, and irrigate it,
To revive its glory and supersede the achievements of those who have taught us.
We shall overcome them with their own weapon,
And the perpetrators shall suffer the consequences of their actions!
We shall return, armed with science and technology!
We shall return with experience and expertise . . .
We shall return. . . . We shall return . . .
And God is our witness!

[*Lights on* DIRECTOR *and* CAMERAMAN.]

DIRECTOR: Good! Fix!

CAMERAMAN: Yes sir!

[*Action freezes.*]

DIRECTOR: Remind me to latch some applause onto this scene. . . . Action!

CAMERAMAN [*pressing buttons on control unit*]: Yes sir!

[*Actors are reanimated.*]

ALL: This is our picture. . . . We transmit it to you with our most distinguished regards.

[*They get into a solid formation symbolizing unity and strength.*]

ALL: Long live Arab unity!

[*The* ANNOUNCERS *appear in the frame, each holding a microphone.*]

M. ANNOUNCER: Fellow citizens . . .

F. ANNOUNCER: This is a wonderful picture, living proof that Arab unity is a glorious and everlasting reality.

M. ANNOUNCER: A picture that does not tell lies, . . . without deceit, without trickery or embellishment.

F. ANNOUNCER: A picture telling us that the great Arab awakening is about to come true.

M. ANNOUNCER: Rather, telling us that the awakening has indeed begun and taken place.

[*An English* POLICEMAN *appears and stops behind the students.*]

M. ANNOUNCER: A picture we place before the arrogant West, which refuses to believe.

F. ANNOUNCER: The West, which paints a distorted and fallacious image of the Arabs.

M. ANNOUNCER: Look at our picture and examine it carefully.

DIRECTOR [*with sudden anger*]: Stop! . . . Stop that tape.

CAMERAMAN [*coolly*]: Yes sir. . . . Don't fret. [*He presses a button and stops action on the stage.*] What's wrong?

DIRECTOR: It's a calamity. Rewind the last two frames and you'll see.

CAMERAMAN: Yes sir. . . . But don't fret!

[*He presses a button and the actors are reanimated, taking one step backwards.*]

DIRECTOR: Look carefully. Can you see the disaster?

CAMERAMAN: No. Where?

DIRECTOR [*sarcastically*]: Your excellency includes the English policeman with them in the picture?

CAMERAMAN: It's him who suddenly appeared while I was filming. But don't fret; we'll cut it out in montage.

DIRECTOR: No good, because you'll cut out the most important shot of the Arabs' picture!

CAMERAMAN: All right then, we'll keep him.

DIRECTOR: No good, because the program is about the struggle of the Arab nation against Western civilization, and the presence of this policeman in this way is really bad!

CAMERAMAN [*impatiently*]: What do you want me to do? We're in England. How do you expect not to see any English policemen?

DIRECTOR: He may be seen, but not above the heads of fourteen youths from fourteen Arab countries. . . . Do you want critics and reporters to tear me to pieces and call me an agent of the West or an ass of a director?

CAMERAMAN: No one would dare call you an agent . . .

DIRECTOR: What??

CAMERAMAN: Don't fret. Gather the Arab youths and I'll film them again for you.

DIRECTOR [*slapping his own face in despair*]: Again? Gather them again?? It has taken me two months to get them together!

[*Dimmed lights*—CAMERAMAN *behind the camera, facing the* ANNOUNCERS *and the* DIRECTOR *in front of the controls unit.*]

F. ANNOUNCER: Dear viewers . . .

DIRECTOR: Cut!

M. ANNOUNCER: Excuse . . .

DIRECTOR: *Cut!*

F. ANNOUNCER: Calm down . . .

M. ANNOUNCER: Don't lose your temper . . .

F. ANNOUNCER: Don't panic!

M. ANNOUNCER: We are forced to present our image to you as perceived through Western eyes; which are, of course, biased against us.

F. ANNOUNCER: For, while at the studio in London preparing this program, which reflects the corruption of the West at its lowest, . . .

M. ANNOUNCER: We were flabbergasted to discover that in the studio next door to us they were filming a program about the ignorance and decadence of the Arabs!

F. ANNOUNCER: Here is a clip from that program.

M. ANNOUNCER: We present it to you in the name of freedom of speech, which we do not fear . . .

[*Film projection: a painted scene of a London street showing Big Ben. A huge-bellied* ARAB MAN *appears, wearing a loose abaya. He wears a face mask with a huge nose and a large mustache. His eyes are protruding and he is followed by four large* WOMEN *conspicuously swaying their fat thighs. Background: old-fashioned Oriental music.*]

DIRECTOR [*tearing off his earphones*]: Stop! . . . Stop that film! [*Immediately, action is frozen onstage.*] No. . . . It pains me to think of airing such a filthy film for everyone to see!

F. ANNOUNCER: We agreed to show only two minutes of the film.

DIRECTOR: It doesn't matter! It's an awful film, degrading the Arabs and depicting them as ignorant savages with no brains!

M. ANNOUNCER: Let everyone see it so that they realize how the West is faking the truth . . .

DIRECTOR: On the contrary! Most people will be taken in by it because they are ignorant. They don't understand.

F. ANNOUNCER: So, what is your answer?

DIRECTOR: Show the film on one condition: that it carries a commentary to warn people and make them aware of the truth.

M. ANNOUNCER: Okay, we're ready.

DIRECTOR [*to the* CAMERAMAN]: Start the film!

[*The actors are reanimated onstage.*]

F. ANNOUNCER: Beware of the trickery of this filthy film!

M. ANNOUNCER: Don't you dare believe it or be taken in by it!

F. ANNOUNCER: You must be irritated and angered by it!

M. ANNOUNCER: Recoil from it in disdain and disgust!

F. ANNOUNCER: It would be advisable not to let your children watch it!

M. ANNOUNCER: And to be on the safe side, don't watch it yourselves!

DIRECTOR: Good. Now I'm in the clear. . . . Sound up!

[*From the other side, another* ARAB MAN *enters, like the first, and they meet in the middle. We hear their conversation. We also hear sporadic canned laughter.*]

FIRST ARAB: My Arab brother!

SECOND ARAB: My Arab brother!

[*They hug.*]

FIRST ARAB: Welcome, welcome, welcome!

SECOND ARAB: Welcome, welcome, welcome!

[*They kiss on the cheeks.*]

FIRST ARAB: By God, I've missed you!

SECOND ARAB: By God, I've missed you!

[*They kiss on the shoulders.*]

FIRST ARAB: How are you?

SECOND ARAB: How are *you*?

[*Energetic handshakes.*]

FIRST ARAB: Fine! Thanks be to God.

SECOND ARAB: Fine! Thanks be to God.

FIRST ARAB: What are you doing here in London?

SECOND ARAB: What are *you* doing here?

FIRST ARAB: By God, I found out that my watch was inaccurate, so I decided to come and buy Big Ben!

SECOND ARAB: And I felt extremely bored, so I decided to come and buy the Tower of London!

FIRST ARAB: May God be with you!

SECOND ARAB: May God be with you! [*Muttering to himself.*] He'll beat me to it and buy the Tower himself!

FIRST ARAB [*muttering to himself*]: He'll beat me to it and buy Big Ben himself!

[*They kiss.*]

FIRST ARAB: God bless you.

SECOND ARAB: God bless you.

FIRST ARAB: Peace be upon you, good-bye.

SECOND ARAB: Peace be upon you . . .

[*Each draws a long dagger from under his abaya and stabs the other in the back.*]

BOTH: Aaaaah! . . . Never mind. . . . God forgives bygone sins!

[*They fall together. The* WOMEN *slap their cheeks and wail. The* POLICEMAN *passes by and dips his fingers in their blood.*]

POLICEMAN [*shocked*]: This isn't blood! It's oil!

THE WOMEN [*in sudden panic*]: God have mercy upon us!

[*Lights out.*]

M. ANNOUNCER: Attention, O Arabs . . .

F. ANNOUNCER: The British newspaper *The Despatch* has published an item today of interest to all Arabs . . .

M. ANNOUNCER: And that is . . . the opening of the latest and most up-to-date nightclub in Europe, . . . the *Pleasure Palace!*

F. ANNOUNCER: Excuse me. . . . Naturally, the news item we are interested in has nothing to do with that brothel!

M. ANNOUNCER: But the article says that the nightclub will turn into a new Arab colony, and demands barring us all from entry!

F. ANNOUNCER: Excuse me. . . . Of course, they mean barring us from entry into the country!

M. ANNOUNCER: And in addition to the article, they have published a large photograph on page three of an Arab . . .

F. ANNOUNCER: Kneeling at the feet of a prostitute . . . and obviously intoxicated.

M. ANNOUNCER: The following report about this story is prepared and presented to you by . . .

F. ANNOUNCER: Sadiqa Salih . . .

M. ANNOUNCER: And Amin Falih . . .

[*The program signature tune and a change in lighting. The* ANNOUNCERS *stand in different corners.*]

DIRECTOR: Stand by. . . . Three . . . two . . . one . . . action!

[STUDENTS *enter*]

M. ANNOUNCER: Mighwar ibn Gabbar, I need your honest opinion. Is there, in the whole Arab nation, anyone who would commit such lunacy?

MIGHWAR: Of course . . . not. The Arabs are enlightened. An Arab would never agree to have himself portrayed in this manner. Most probably he was treacherously filmed in a moment of total unawareness. . . . Buddy, he was as drunk as a skunk! [*Exit.*]

F. ANNOUNCER: Brother Antar Abu Khangar, isn't it your opinion as well . . .

ANTAR [*interrupting*]: No. The admission of truth is a virtue. The publicized image is truthful and depicts someone we know very well from a brotherly country dear to us all. He is from . . .

DIRECTOR: Stop! Don't identify the country.

ANTAR: If you want honest opinions, let us speak. . . . There is no need for exaggerated sensitivities.

F. ANNOUNCER: Are we producing a program to rally the Arabs together, or to break them apart?

DIRECTOR: Okay. . . . Let him speak his mind, Professor Sadiqa. [*He whispers to the* CAMERAMAN *in his microphone.*] Can you hear me?

CAMERAMAN: Yes.

DIRECTOR: Film him, and when he names the country I'll kill the sound!

F. ANNOUNCER: Go ahead, brother Antar . . .

ANTAR: That country, specifically, is . . . . [*He moves his lips but we cannot hear him. Exit.*]

M. ANNOUNCER: Brother Khuzaa, what is your reaction to brother Antar's opinion?

KHUZAA: It doesn't matter which country, we are all together in misery. But whoever chooses to expose his kin and his people shall, by the will of God, be exposed and humiliated together with his whole family . . . [*Exit.*]

DIRECTOR: *Cut!*

F. ANNOUNCER: Sister Rabha, allow me to ask you: If a young man like the one whose photograph is published in the paper proposed to you, would you agree to marry him . . . if he were the last man on earth?

RABHA: Never! These young men our nation is damned with throw themselves at the feet of foreign women and abandon their own and let them turn into dried prunes, spinsters!

DIRECTOR: *Cut!* [*Exit* RABHA.]

M. ANNOUNCER: Brother Adham, do you approve of frequenting a shady venue like the Pleasure Palace? Of course not. . . . Thank you for this honest opinion!

ADHAM: Excuse me. [*Exit.*]

DIRECTOR: *Stop!* Call him back, quickly!

M. ANNOUNCER: Brother Adham! . . . [*To the* DIRECTOR.] What's wrong?

DIRECTOR: The man hasn't answered yet!

M. ANNOUNCER: Really? Sorry, I didn't notice.

DIRECTOR: Brother Adham, we are sorry. . . . As soon as we start filming, your honor replies and says *"Of course not!"*

ADHAM: Of course not.

DIRECTOR [*shouting*]: Not yet, man! . . . Wait until we say "We are filming." . . . We are filming!

ADHAM: Of course not. [*Exit.*]

F. ANNOUNCER: Brethren Luqman and Simaan, sons of Soliman, would you advise your brothers to frequent a filthy, infested place like the Pleasure Palace, where they would spend all the money needed by their country?

BOTH TOGETHER: God, no! . . . Of course not!

LUQMAN: Because this Pleasure Palace is no ordinary nightclub.

SIMAAN: This is a supermarket nightclub!

LUQMAN: Inside are forty rooms . . . Wow! *Plenty of room for dancing!* . . .

SIMAAN: And plenty of room for . . . making out . . .

LUQMAN: A room for alcohol . . . and a room for heroin . . .

SIMAAN: And a room for broads . . . and a room for young men . . .

LUQMAN: That is besides ten gambling halls, . . . blue movies, . . . and live striptease shows. . . . Briefly, all means of amusement and pleasure and happiness and merriment and fun to satisfy all tastes! . . . [*Sobering.*] But of course, they all invoke the wrath of God, and that is why I warn my brethren against frequenting such places . . .

BOTH: Especially as entry is free, no ticket or fee required!

DIRECTOR: Hell! . . . This is a plug! . . .

CAMERAMAN [*leaves the camera and follows* LUQMAN]: Brother! . . . Mate, . . . are you sure entry is free?!

LUQMAN: Of course, mate. [*Exeunt* LUQMAN *and* SIMAAN.]

CAMERAMAN: Shame on you all! Free entry and you never told me, all this time?!

DIRECTOR: Don't fret.

CAMERAMAN: I am fretting. And by God, I'm not working anymore. Huh!

DIRECTOR: Don't be so childish! Is this just spite, . . . silly revenge?

CAMERAMAN: I would cut off my arm to prove that you've been there behind my back!

M. ANNOUNCER: Are we stupid or what?? True, entrance is free . . . but inside, temptation makes you forget your people; and you pay for it with your own blood.

CAMERAMAN: They say "Enjoy watching what you can't afford to buy." What do you want me to say when I go back home and they ask me what I've seen? Do you want me to say *nothing?!*

F. ANNOUNCER [*sarcastic, secretly filming him*]: Bravo! That's a straight, brave opinion!

M. ANNOUNCER: Brother Lutfi, what is your opinion of the reality of the Arab nation?

CAMERAMAN: The reality of the Arab nation is mud and more mud!

M. ANNOUNCER [*bringing the microphone closer*]: Don't you agree with me that Arab unity could . . .

CAMERAMAN [*excited*]: Whose unity, buddy? Do you believe newspapers and TV? Please don't urge me to blurt it out! [*Facing the camera.*]: Have you been recording this?

M. ANNOUNCER: Mr. Director, what do you say to broadcasting this sequence?

DIRECTOR: Are you crazy?

M. ANNOUNCER: What's wrong? For once, we include an opposing point of view.

F. ANNOUNCER: Imagine the viewers when they hear what Lutfi said.

CAMERAMAN: But this talk is not allowed!

M. ANNOUNCER: But you said it, Mister, and it's been recorded!

DIRECTOR: It can be said among ourselves, but not broadcast!

CAMERAMAN: I'm doomed!

F. ANNOUNCER: If we'd specified, from the start, what to say
and what not to say, why are we asking people then? If we
are going to air some interviews and bury others, then why
do we ask people to watch our program? . . . Answer me
that! . . .

DIRECTOR: Because you can't convey the truth on camera!

CAMERAMAN: You don't like us, then? Just show me the truth
and I'll get it on film!

DIRECTOR: I mean that as soon as an Arab sees a camera he
immediately goes into a schizophrenic trance and says anything but what he really feels.

CAMERAMAN: Easy! We use a hidden camera. It's as small as my
palm. I hide it in my pocket, and no one will know I'm filming. But I get a bonus for this!

DIRECTOR: Hell! Do you want to ruin us? Does anyone in this
day and age tell people the truth to their face?

M. ANNOUNCER: Listen, buddy, all the Arab ministers took the
decision together to make this program and they signed
official statements that it's not subject to any censoring authority.

CAMERAMAN: And you really believe that?

F. ANNOUNCER: Do *not* forget that for three months this program has been presented each week by a crew from a different country. . . . Do you want them to say the Egyptians
are the cowards who panicked? That they are the ones who
have no democracy and no freedom of speech?

M. ANNOUNCER: I swear by my mother's life—which I never do
lightly—that I am taking no part in the production of this
program unless I am fully convinced of every word in it.

F. ANNOUNCER: I am with you, Amin, and let them rant and
swear as much as they like!

DIRECTOR: Of course, you're newly engaged and are about to
get married. But I have children. Have mercy!

M. ANNOUNCER: Come off it! [*He turns to the camera, smiling.*]
Dear viewers . . .

F. ANNOUNCER: Your program, "In Plain Arabic" . . .

M. ANNOUNCER: Offers you sincere apologies . . .

F. ANNOUNCER: For all that we have presented so far.

M. ANNOUNCER: We pledge, from this moment on . . .

F. ANNOUNCER: To abide by honesty, truth, and accuracy! And as the truth is relative . . .

M. ANNOUNCER: Let us regard this program purely as an Egyptian point of view . . .

F. ANNOUNCER: Sorry—it's not just one point of view, but *four* Egyptian points of view . . .

M. ANNOUNCER: Concerning the Arab cause in general . . . and our struggle against Western civilization.

Lights out.

SCENE I

Lobby in a small London hotel. Main door, reception desk, and access to the management. A side passage leads to the rooms on the ground floor; some of the doors can be seen. Opposite side: staircase leading to the upper floor. Several more doors. Simple furniture: a couch, several poufs, bean bags, and a small table. A door marked BAR. Tourist posters on the walls. Time: Autumn evening. STUDENTS *on seats and mats. Some are smoking waterpipes. One is playing the lute accompanying a girl supported by the students' chorus. All sound is subdued, as if the director had complete control over the volume.* ANNOUNCERS *heard over the music.*

M. ANNOUNCER: Is it true that Arabs are united only in sorrow?

F. ANNOUNCER: We have taken the opportunity of our blessed Feast, the breaking of the Ramadan fast, to put this question to you.

M. ANNOUNCER: The camera is now moving into the hotel where our students are staying.

F. ANNOUNCER: Our students have organized an Arab evening to celebrate our Feast!

M. ANNOUNCER: Our hidden candid camera—unbeknownst to all—recorded the following footage . . .

F. ANNOUNCER: But little did we know that we had stumbled onto such a juicy story!

[GEORGE, *behind reception desk handling orders.*]

GEORGE: Happy Feast! Can I be of any help?

KHUZAA: George, thank you!

[*Enter other students.*]

SAKHR: God's blessings and a Happy Feast!

YAZID: Health and blessings to all!

KHUZAA: May God protect you from all evil!

MIGHWAR: May all your days be blessed!

SAYF: God's blessings . . . God's greetings to you all!

[GEORGE *stares at them in amazement as they all hug.*]

SAKHR: What's your problem, Mr. George? We Arabs love each other, because we are blood brothers.

ANTAR: What is *your* problem, Sakhr? Do you have to give him a running commentary?

SAKHR: No, but foreigners are not familiar with our overflowing emotions, and they think badly of men who hug and kiss!

YAZID: By God! Aren't they backward!

JASIR: Greetings brothers! [*To* ADHAM.] You're not done yet with the decorations?

ADHAM: Khuzaa was supposed to buy them and he didn't.

KHUZAA: If I go shopping in my Arab headdress and robe the prices will rocket sky high. I sent Luqman instead. . . . He's good at bargaining and he looks like a heathen Westerner!

LUQMAN: We are a nation of shrewd tradesmen. I've been to the remotest marketplace and bought everything at bottom price.

KHUZAA: Great! This means that you still have some change left?

LUQMAN: Of course, buddy. . . . Of course I did.

KHUZAA: Where is it then?

LUQMAN: Hey, chum! I used it on transport!

JASIR: But these are western decorations; not oriental or Arab.

LUQMAN: Man! What are you talking about? We're here in London. . . . By your sister's life, where do you want me to find Arab decorations?

[*Enter* HIKMAT.]

HIKMAT: What's with you guys? You're always fighting like angry roosters!

KHUZAA: You've come at the right time. . . . Here, get the place ready and serve us.

RABHA: What's with you men? Whenever you see us we have to work?

KHUZAA [*retreating*]: I didn't mean *you!*

[MUSTAFA appears in his pajamas, swaying an incense burner.]

MUSTAFA: In the name of God . . . Praise be to God, the Almighty. . . . We all gather in the company of our Prophet with the blessing of God, the One and Only. . . . And may He blind him who does not pray for our Prophet! [*Exit.*]

MIGHWAR: A dollop of discipline before we start our evening! Let me remind you of our long-standing agreement: *No* discussion of religion, *no* discussion of ancestry and descent, *no* discussion of politics . . . we do *not* want to hurt anybody's feelings.

HIKMAT: We demand an addition to the restrictions.

SAYF: What would that be, sister Hikmat?

HIKMAT [*to* RABHA]: *You* say.

RABHA: No, sis, . . . *you* say.

JASIR: Understood. . . . No discussion of sex. We have women here!

SOME [*laughing*]: Agreed. God be our Judge!

SAYF: Thanks be to God. . . . As long as we don't get physical, we shall never disagree. . . . There is *nothing to disagree about!*

TAMMAM [*his ear stuck to the radio, suddenly shouting*]: God is Great! . . . I thank You, *God!* [*Dances madly.*] We have won! We are heroes!

MUSTAFA: My heartiest congratulations Tammam. . . . What have you won?

TAMMAM: We have achieved our ultimate aim. We have achieved world fame. We have entered . . .

ANTAR: *Israel?*

TAMMAM: The World Cup!

MUSTAFA: Although I know nothing about soccer, . . . congratulations! [*He hugs him.*] And who have you defeated?

TAMMAM: We have defeated you! We scored a goal against you! Against your country!

MUSTAFA: Go to Hell! . . . You don't even know how to play. We taught you everything!

[*Action freezes with no sound. Violent fist fight noises.* ANNOUNCERS' *voices.*]

F. ANNOUNCER: On this special occasion, they had invited their university professor, . . .

M. ANNOUNCER: Professor Richard Wisdom, an orientalist and master of the Arabic language.

[*Enter* PROF. WISDOM *unnoticed in the hubbub of the fight.*]

SU'DUD: So what? We beat you in fifty-one!

RABHA: Okay, guys! *No* discussion of soccer either!

ANTAR: Shame on you, by God! The foreigner is coming. What would he say if he saw you?

[*They all shut up as they realize* PROF. WISDOM's *presence.*]

ANTAR: Do I have to scream at you to make you pull yourselves together?! Had it not been for this chaos, we would have . . .

PROF. WISDOM: Peace be upon you all!

ANTAR [*embarrassed*]: Professor Wisdom, welcome! We are honored!

PROF. WISDOM: Thank you, thank you. It is my great pleasure. [*Sits on a cushion on the floor.*]

RABHA: What would you like to drink, Professor?

PROF. WISDOM: A cup of tea, if you please.

RABHA: We have great Arabic coffee.

PROF. WISDOM: A cup of tea, if you please.

HIKMAT: We also have cinnamon and ginger and hibiscus tea and caraway and tamarind and carob.

PROF. WISDOM: Thank you . . . a cup of tea . . . if you please!

SU'DUD: We would have liked to offer you spirits, but our traditions don't allow us.

ADHAM: But it is possible. We can get George to serve it to you.

PROF. WISDOM: Thank you. A cup of tea, if you please.

RABHA: Good, here we are . . . the coffee is ready. [*She pours for* PROF. WISDOM.]

LUQMAN: And the water-pipe as well.

HIKMAT: I implore you to have a taste of my biscuits.

RABHA: We must know what you think of Arabic food.

PROF. WISDOM [*with horror*]: But you come from twenty-one different countries, with different types of food!

MUSTAFA: We're celebrating. The fast has ended and today is our feast!

PROF. WISDOM: I know, today you go back to normal eating.

MUSTAFA: Exactly.

PROF. WISDOM: That is, you don't eat as much as you did during Ramadan, your fasting month.

ALL: *What?*

LAYTH: Even you, our professor, have the wrong idea about us, like all other Westerners.

PROF. WISDOM: Not at all! You know I sympathize with most of your causes, and I appreciate and value the Eastern heritage.

LAYTH: That's why we came to you. We have written a research about the image of the Arabs as it is mutilated by European media, and we want it published in the English papers.

PROF. WISDOM: The papers won't publish it unless it's a paid advertisement.

ADHAM [*heatedly*]: We'll pay, . . . whatever the price. We are ready to give our last penny!

SAYF [*annoyed*]: Excuse me, buddy, . . . how much money have you got in your pocket?

ADHAM: The brethren have money, and we are all together!

KHUZAA: Look at me! . . . Isn't it enough I had to pay through the nose last week when you insisted I had to buy all the copies of that anti-Arab book to prevent anyone from reading it?

PROF. WISDOM [*laughing*]: Wonderful!

KHUZAA: And what came of it? They thought the book was a bestseller . . . and they printed more copies!

SAKHR: It's that bookshop in Piccadilly. It always publishes books against us.

PROF. WISDOM: I don't think so. Actually, it publishes books with a variety of viewpoints.

MUSTAFA: That's why we decided to react to this mutilated image the West paints of our people.

SAKHR: We decided that the best way to express our unity as Arab brothers would be a play.

PROF. WISDOM: A play?

SAKHR: Yes indeed. A play, written by me, called "Woe, Ye Arabs." It's excellent!

MUSTAFA: And I am the director, also in charge of casting.

SAKHR: The main point is that it exposes all foreigners and brings all your defects to light! We have high hopes in you, Professor, to help stage it at the university.

PROF. WISDOM: But I haven't read it yet.

SAKHR: I'll tell you. The hero is a youth from an Arab tribe. He is abducted by an English imperialist who wants the whole tribe to submit to his terms.

MUSTAFA: Naturally, the abducted youth is a symbol of the Palestinian cause! Are you with me?

PROF. WISDOM: And how does the play end?

SAKHR: I haven't thought it out yet. But, naturally, it has to be a happy ending.

PROF. WISDOM: God willing!

SAKHR: God willing, he is rescued by one of his brethren.

PROF. WISDOM: And who plays the youth?

MUSTAFA: Brother Fayez. But he isn't here right now.

PROF. WISDOM: And who plays the rescuer?

ALL: I do!! [*They look at each other.*]

HIKMAT [*staring at the entrance*]: My God! Brother Fayez! He's here! He's hurt! He's bleeding!

[*Enter* FAYEZ, *face bloodstained.*]

ALL: Fayez! . . . What happened to you?!

[*Action freezes.* ANNOUNCERS' *voices.*]

M. ANNOUNCER: Dear viewers . . .

F. ANNOUNCER: Pardon the interruption . . .

M. ANNOUNCER: That was the beginning of the story . . .

F. ANNOUNCER: Which we have decided to follow to the end.

HIKMAT [*trying to keep them away from* FAYEZ]: Don't smother him! Let him catch his breath!

RABHA: How did you get hurt? Were you in a fight?

FAYEZ [*moaning*]: Yes. They trapped me. . . . I was all alone.

LAYTH: You are among your brothers. You are never alone.

MUSTAFA: He who sprays you with water, we spray with *blood!*

ANTAR: Tell me who hassled you and I will grind him to dust then slash his throat!

SAKHR: You cut his throat on your own? Do you think you are the only tough one around?

LUQMAN: I'll slay him for you, buddy, in broad daylight! [*He draws a gun.*]

YAZID: Who is the miserable creature? [*He draws a dagger.*]

SU'DUD: Sugar, Fayez . . . what happened to you?

FAYEZ: On my way here I ran into a bunch of English derelicts near Piccadilly Circus. . . . They said, "Come over here, let's have a talk." I refused . . .

JASIR: Have a talk about what?

FAYEZ: I don't know. I really didn't want any argument at all, and when I came to leave, one of them insulted me.

MUSTAFA: Son of a bitch! What did he say?

FAYEZ: I wish he had insulted me alone . . . but he insulted you all!

ALL: *How?*

FAYEZ [*agonizing*]: He said . . . You . . . You . . .

ALL: You *what?*

FAYEZ [*almost in tears*]: You . . . *Arab!*

ALL [*in protest*]: *What?* He called you an *Arab?!*

FAYEZ: By God, yes . . . and he repeated it three times for all to hear!

MUSTAFA: And you did nothing?

FAYEZ: No, I sprang at him with blood boiling in my veins.

HIKMAT: And then?

FAYEZ: All of a sudden, I was flat on the floor, with blood pouring *out* of my veins.

PROF. WISDOM: Friends, allow me to explain that the word "Arab" is not meant as an insult. It is merely a descriptive term, no more and no less.

ADHAM [*exclaiming in sudden recognition*]: By God! You're absolutely right! We are actually Arabs!

SAYF [*to* FAYEZ]: Why then were you offended? Are you denying your Arab ancestry? Do you consider it a humiliating stigma?

[ALL mumbling together, denigrating FAYEZ's reaction.]

FAYEZ: Listen to me! [*Seems to suddenly recognize the reason for his anger.*] He threw it at me as an insult or a damnation! A spell! He threw it at me with total scorn. It flew out of his lips like spit in my face. He meant you beast, backward savage, uncivilized creature! Everyone there laughed at me!

SAYF: Tell me, were there any females?

FAYEZ: Yeah! Of course!

SAYF: Then, brethren . . . it is revenge or disgrace!

ADHAM: All foreigners are a lowly race!

HIKMAT [*whispering*]: We forgot about the professor. [*To* FAYEZ.] Come, Fayez, let's first clean your wounds.

[*Exeunt* HIKMAT, RABHA, *and* FAYEZ *to his room.*]

PROF. WISDOM: I have a suggestion: Fayez could have answered this person who called him an Arab by saying "What's your problem, you Western European," and that would have put an end to the crisis.

JASIR: You are an idealist, Professor. Leave this matter to us, we'll handle it our own way.

[*They all gather in one corner and whisper animatedly.*]

LUQMAN: Professor, have something to drink. By the life of me, you must have something to drink.

PROF. WISDOM [*startled*]: No . . . no . . . thank you. I must leave.

MUSTAFA [*taking him to the door*]: Why so soon, Professor? . . . By God, you must stay longer . . .

SOME [*in anger*]: Vengeance . . . Vengeance, brethren!

MUSTAFA: Vengeance? . . . By God, guys, calm down and let's think this over properly.

LUQMAN: Yes. We must find this guy and discuss matters with him.

SAKHR [*interrupting*]: We have nothing to discuss with this sort of people. We have nothing to discuss.

TAMMAM: Pourquoi? We beat him with our argument and retrieve our Arab rights.

KHUZAA: How? . . . Suppose he beats us in the argument and we find that he is in the right. . . . How would you like that?

LUQMAN: In such a case, we beat him to death, and it would be well deserved.

ANTAR: Indeed. This is a matter of principle. Our student grants administration warned me. "When you go to the West," they said, "don't you dare argue with anybody, or allow anyone to argue with you."

ADHAM: Understood. But now we are not at home. I mean, nobody can see us.

SAKHR [*whispering*]: How do you know nobody can hear us?

MUSTAFA: Listen, gentlemen, this is not a question of power and prowess. We are in their country, they are the majority. Our reply to them has to be civilized. We must teach them a lesson and show them how Arabs think.

LUQMAN: Like how?

MUSTAFA [*confused*]: Huh? I don't know. But we must think . . .

SAKHR: Enough talk, brothers. Enough humiliation, enough degradation.

JASIR: This is the moment for serious action.

TAMMAM: A slap in the face cannot be met by arguments.

LAYTH: A slap in the face has to be returned.

ADHAM: Today. At this hour. *Now*.

MIGHWAR: Immediately. This instant. Not tomorrow.

ALL [*excited*]: Now. *Now*. Not tomorrow.

ANTAR: A cutting reply, a glorious act . . . on top of their heads!

ALL: Today. This instant. Now. Not tomorrow. Not tomorrow.

ANTAR: And if you fear the battle, stay behind, we can handle it.

MUSTAFA: Afraid? Me? I swear by all the grace and blessings of God that no one will avenge Fayez's honor but me, and me alone!

JASIR: He has full right. Allow him the opportunity to avenge Fayez's honor by himself.

LUQMAN: May God be with you.

MUSTAFA: What's this? Every time you get fired up, then you turn tail?

KHUZAA: You wish to fight them with words?

MUSTAFA: Not another word. I am very capable and you all know it.

SAKHR: By God, we won't allow you to enjoy this honor alone!

ANTAR: No sir indeed. We follow your every step, and outdo your every action.

MUSTAFA: Let's all take a vow to put our hands together and achieve what the governments have failed to accomplish.

SAKHR and ANTAR [*together*]: Yes indeed, what your governments have failed to accomplish!

JASIR: Agreed. S'il vous plaît, hands together, gentlemen. Let's recite the Fatiha!

[*They all put their right hands on top of his, except* LUQMAN.]

SAYF: And why are you standing aside and not reciting the Fatiha with us?

LUQMAN: I am Luqman, buddy!

SAYF: Luqman, so what? What's special about you?

LUQMAN: Luqman, cousin. . . . Luqman, son of Soliman the Maronite Christian. . . . Get it?

SAYF: And how did that come about?

LUQMAN: God's will!

ALL [*as they finish reciting the Fatiha*]: Amen!

SAKHR: Men! Together we shall avenge Fayez and take revenge on those who humiliated him and beat him up.

[HIKMAT *and* RABHA *return.*]

HIKMAT: Men, take us with you.

KHUZAA: Women have nothing to do with battles and wars.

RABHA: How come foreign women fight side by side with their men? You don't lack courage or faith, but foreigners always get the best of us; so what is it that you're lacking? Us: Arab women!

KHUZAA: Never mind, all right. Come on, quickly now!

RABHA: Wha . . . ? Give us time to freshen up our makeup! [*Exit with* HIKMAT.]

[*The phone rings.* GEORGE *answers, speaks for a short while, then hangs up.*]

GEORGE: There's a huge party at the Pleasure Palace tonight. They called to ask if anyone would like to go.

[ALL *turn away from him in disdain.*]

GEORGE: This is a special party, with fancy dress and masks that hide your identity!

SAYF: May God protect us from these satanic thoughts.

[*Suddenly, everybody is quiet.*]

SU'DUD: I say, it would be better to postpone Fayez's business until tomorrow!

ADHAM: By God, you're right. . . . We rest tonight and tomorrow morning we'll be in tiptop shape.

ANTAR: Done. We meet tomorrow at eleven and we go to Piccadilly Circus and attack the enemy with our full might.

MUSTAFA: With God's blessing. Indeed, "Haste is from the Devil."

KHUZAA: Come on! Let's have some music . . . the night is still young.

ANTAR [*to* TAMMAM—*sternly*]: Sing!

TAMMAM [*starts to sing*]: *Ya weeli yaaba ya weeli . . .*

KHUZAA [*suddenly*]: Excuse me, brothers, I have a headache and I'm in real pain! [*Exit.*]

MUSTAFA: Bless him. Me too . . . I don't know what's the matter with me. [*Exit.*]

SAYF: I'm going for my evening prayers and I'll be right back. Promise. [*Exit.*]

LUQMAN: I have to finish a few letters to my family and friends. [*Exit.*]

SAKHR: I have to spend some time on my own and revise the play I'm writing. [*Exit.*]

SU'DUD [*carrying his food*]: I am going to look for something to eat! [*Exit.*]

ANTAR: I would rather go to bed, I am not feeling very well! [*Exit.*]

ADHAM: By God, good idea! [*Exit.*]

[MIGHWAR *mumbles incomprehensibly. Exit.*]

YAZID: I feel exactly the same!

JASIR [*angrily to the rest*]: What are you sitting here for? Why don't you leave too?!

LAYTH: Are you staying?

JASIR: No, I'm out, in protest against this chaos! [*Exit.*]

TAMMAM: I'm going straight to my room to study. [*Exit.*]

GEORGE [*on his way out*]: Good night.

LAYTH [*with sudden understanding*]: Oooh! . . . And I forgot I had an urgent appointment! [*Rushes out.*]

[*The stage is deserted. Sound of the radio.*]

VOICE: This is London. The Arabic service of the BBC wishes its distinguished listeners a happy and blessed Feast.

[*FAYEZ appears and stands in the spotlight looking around him in confusion.*]

FAYEZ: Where did they all go, leaving me all alone?

[*Arabic song on the radio. Gradually, loud pop music drowns the Arabic song.*]

Gradual lights out.

SCENE II

Inside a discotheque. Background made up of several doors leading to other rooms. Signs on the doors saying BAR, DRUGS, GAMES, GIRLS, BOYS. Mysterious atmosphere: strobe lights, thick smoke, surrealistic decor, loud music, hysterical laughter. In the spotlight, someone wearing a crying mask, confused, bumping into dancers. When he turns around we realize that he had been standing with his back to us. Now we see the other side of the mask: a smiling face. Light gradually up revealing the other dancers, some wearing masks of politicians like Bush, Thatcher, Gorbachev, Mitterand, and Kohl. One is dressed like an English POLICEMAN and moves exactly like one. Some people enter alone, wearing different masks. They appear nervous, then gradually relax and gather to the right of the stage. CAMERAMAN enters, carrying a small video camera; he tries to hide it and film the scene. SUPERVISOR passes through and signals with his hand. Music stops and changes to a serene tango. The group on the right rush to dance with the girls, elbowing each other. They dance in a tight embrace. One in a ROMEO *mask stands with a* JULIET *in the foreground.*

ROMEO: I love you.

JULIET: I love you, too.

ROMEO: And I hate Arabs.

JULIET: Oh, me too.

TOGETHER: Thank God!

[*Both shocked.*]

ROMEO: Are you . . . ?

JULIET: Are you . . . ?

[*They run away from each other.*]

SUPERVISOR [*through the microphone*]: A special request for our friends.

[*The music of an Arabic song, "We want to get married during the Feast." Some of the group on the right gradually join the dance. A* GIRL *starts belly dancing, a* MAN *drums the beat for her and offers her a necklace of dollar bills. Lights and music change. Everybody appears tired and drunk. A* WOMAN *in an animal mask appears and begins to strip.* ALL *gather around her. Suddenly all lights are out for a brief moment. When they come on again, the stripper has disappeared and* TWO MEN *in cowboy clothes, each holding two guns, appear.* ALL *laugh and applaud. But the men fire in the air.* ALL *terrified; the air is electrified with fear.*]

FIRST ROBBER: This is an armed robbery!

SECOND ROBBER: Hand in all your money and jewelry. Quick, or I take your life!

[ALL *hand in a handful of bills in hesitation. The fake* POLICEMAN *stands still. Someone trips the* FIRST ROBBER *with his foot; he loses his balance.* ALL *get embroiled in fist fights in slow motion. Lights out for a brief moment. Lights. The* POLICEMAN, *now revealed to be a* THIRD ROBBER, *is holding all at gunpoint.*]

THIRD ROBBER: Face to the wall and hands up. Try anything funny and I'll shoot.

[ALL *obey, turning their backs to the audience. The group wearing politicians' masks watches in silence.*]

THIRD ROBBER: Take off those masks!

[ALL *obey quickly, but each is wearing a white featureless mask underneath.*]

THIRD ROBBER: All of you! Remove the second mask!

[ALL *hold on to their masks, moaning in supplication.*]

THIRD ROBBER [*laughs, then shouts*]: Hurry or I'll take your mask. . . . Your money or your mask!

[*Immediately,* ALL *hand over their money and remove their watches and rings.*]

Gradual lights out.

SCENE III

At the studio.

M. ANNOUNCER: Next day, the morning papers published an item which rocked the whole of Britain.

F. ANNOUNCER: The story was . . .

M. ANNOUNCER: Last night, an unidentified person broke into a bookshop in Piccadilly and destroyed all its contents using a fire bomb.

F. ANNOUNCER: The public demands the immediate arrest and trial of the perpetrator.

M. ANNOUNCER: As for what transpired that night in the Pleasure Palace, it was published in small print in the evening papers, thus attracting the attention of few readers.

Inside the hotel.

[GEORGE *is reading the papers while listening to soft music on the radio.* MUSTAFA *rushes out of his room in his pajamas.*]

MUSTAFA: George . . . what time is it?

GEORGE: It's five past two.

MUSTAFA: Why did you let me sleep until five past two? Why didn't you wake me up?

GEORGE: I tried, not once but twice. Every time you tell me "Leave me five more minutes."

MUSTAFA: And you go along with me? How can I ever face my friends? They must all be gone . . . our meeting was at eleven.

GEORGE: I haven't seen anything at all.

MUSTAFA: They'll gloat in my humiliation. They'll call me a coward, a defeatist, and who knows what else! . . . By the way, you didn't see me yesterday.

GEORGE: What?

MUSTAFA: Look, here, take this.

[*Gives him money.*]

GEORGE: Thank you.

MUSTAFA: You didn't see me yesterday when I went out and returned at dawn. O.K.?

GEORGE: My dear friend. I haven't seen anything at all.

MUSTAFA: Shall I consider this our secret, George?

GEORGE: Mister Mustafa, I am an honest man and I cannot lie. I cannot snitch. I cannot accept bribes . . .

MUSTAFA: I trust your integrity George. I must quickly put my clothes on and catch up with them . . . they must be fighting and needing me.

[*Enter* MARGARET.]

MARGARET: Mustafa, darling.

MUSTAFA: Margaret! What are you doing here now?

MARGARET: Darling, you asked me to meet you.

MUSTAFA: Oh. But this is an emergency. My buddies are fighting a group of delinquent English kids and I must go and punch with them.

MARGARET: Shall I come and punch with you, darling?

MUSTAFA: But they're your compatriots, from your neighborhood, Margaret!

MARGARET: Now *you* are my people, Mustafa. And since they've upset your friends I must give them hell. Let's go! [*She hollers, pulling up her sleeves.*] Yahoo!

MUSTAFA [*moves toward the exit then stops in his tracks*]: I'm not dressed yet!

[*Exeunt* MUSTAFA *and* MARGARET *to Mustafa's room as antar enters from the other side.*]

ANTAR [*looks around then goes to* GEORGE *and whispers*]: George.

GEORGE: Yes?

[ANTAR *whispers something in his ear.*]

GEORGE: Mr. Antar . . . I am an honest man. I cannot lie. I cannot snitch. I cannot accept bribes!

ANTAR [*handing him money*]: Here.

GEORGE: Thank you.

[*Enter* SAKHR.]

SAKHR: Sleep like an angel, brother Antar?

ANTAR [*nervously*]: I have been up for quite a while.

SAKHR: How strange, in spite of being with me last night till dawn!

ANTAR: I? With you where?

SAKHR: In my sleep, buddy! True, your face looked different. But the voice was exactly yours.

ANTAR: A piece of advice, brother: forget all your dreams as soon as you wake up.

[*Enter* ADHAM, *singing*.]

ADHAM: *We want to get married at the feast . . .* [*Sees them. Pauses a moment then sings an Arabic anthem:*] *My beloved homeland, day after day your glories increase!*

[*Others enter one by one, looking exhausted. Then the girls enter.*]

RABHA: Greetings.

KHUZAA [*in disdain*]: Even you, girls? Even you?

RABHA [*attacking*]: Even us *what?*

KHUZAA [*sweetly*]: You arrive late.

RABHA: We don't have the same rights you have? You even want us to justify our sleep?

HIKMAT: I had a nightmare. I dreamt I was robbed then when I woke up I couldn't find my one and only gold chain!

SAYF: God will compensate you for your loss. Patience is a virtue . . .

[GEORGE *suddenly laughs as he reads the paper.*]

JASIR [*angrily*]: Do I look funny? Are you making fun of me?

SAYF: He's not laughing at you, pal, he's laughing at me!

GEORGE [*surprised*]: I'm laughing at the news in the paper.

SAKHR: Tell us. Make us laugh with you.

GEORGE: Last night there was a big robbery at the Pleasure Palace.

ANTAR [*surprised*]: Wow! It is already printed? [*He realizes what he's saying and stops.*]

GEORGE: The thieves robbed many patrons. They took their money and their watches and their gold and their diamonds . . . they took it all . . . all!

ADHAM [*worried*]: Have the police identified the . . . [*He hesitates.*]

GEORGE: Robbers?

ALL [*anxiously*]: No . . . the patrons!

GEORGE: No, that's the problem. Nobody has filed any complaint with the police. That's why they had to release the robbers.

ALL: How odd!

LUQMAN: Drop this subject and let's concentrate on real business. We had an appointment today.

ADHAM: Yes, we agreed to do the play today . . . I mean rehearsal.

SAKHR [*pulling out papers*]: Would you like me to read you the scene I wrote this morning?

[MUSTAFA *peeks from behind.*]

ALL [*feebly, not wanting to hear the play*]: Ohhhh . . .

MUSTAFA [*to himself*]: They must have been savagely beaten! [*He sneaks out.*]

SAKHR [*reading*]: No matter what . . . we shall sacrifice our blood, and death to all cowards.

ALL [*applauding sympathetically*]: God is Great!

MUSTAFA [*to himself, with shame*]: Tsk, tsk. . . . They're talking about me in my absence.

ANTAR [*seeing him*]: Brother Mustafa.

MUSTAFA [*turns around swiftly as if he had just arrived; accusingly*]: Your majesties, where have you been?? I went to meet you in Piccadilly Circus. Not one of you was there!

[ALL *exchange looks then look at him.*]

MUSTAFA [*nervously*]: What are you looking at me like that for? Yes, I went . . . but a little late.

ANTAR: Some unforeseen circumstances stopped us from going.

MUSTAFA [*baffled*]: What are you saying? All of you?

LUQMAN: What's with you, brother? We just told you. Anyone can stumble into unforeseen circumstances. . . . Have you no mercy?

JASIR: And the battle can be postponed to a more convenient time.

[MUSTAFA *laughs uncontrollably.*]

SAKHR: What's this guy laughing for?

ANTAR: He is laughing at us, as usual.

MUSTAFA [*with sudden revelation, attacking*]: Stop it, enough! You dare utter one word after you left me to fight forty men in an uneven battle?

RABHA: And what did you do?

MUSTAFA: I struggled as much as I could. I hit seven with my right and nine with my left and I headbutted two or three.

HIKMAT: Poor you! . . . No wonder you're wounded. [*Points at a scratch on his face.*]

MUSTAFA: Yes! And they also robbed me. They took everything I own, my watch, my wallet, and even the amulet I was carrying in memory of my dear late mother!

ALL [*together, suspiciously*]: How odd!

MUSTAFA: No matter . . . let's stick to the other play . . . [*Shouts.*] Rehearsal!

MARGARET: Mustafa, where have you been, my darling?

HIKMAT: What was *she* doing in your room?

MUSTAFA [*indignantly*]: What? I was training her for a part with us in the play!

ANTAR [*sarcastically*]: "I fought seven with my right and nine with my left!?"

HIKMAT: Lousy play! And I thought you were exhausted from the battle.

MARGARET: Yeah, I'm going punching with you.

HIKMAT: May God punch you in your heart! All of you! [*She retreats to her room with* RABHA.]

MUSTAFA: Margaret, go now and I'll call you.

MARGARET: Okay, see you! [*She kisses him and leaves.*]

SAYF: How can you pretend that foreigners are your enemies when you want to be one of the family?

MUSTAFA: Listen here, don't push your luck. I don't love her. I'm just having fun with her.

ANTAR: And you say it with no shame?

ADHAM: By God he's right. What has the man got to lose?

SAKHR: This is a matter of principles which cannot be isolated. If it's a sin to cheat with Arab women then . . .

SAYF [*interrupting*]: No, with their fallen, sinful, blond broads there is no sin! And you are fully entitled to put your hands on any woman of this kind!

MUSTAFA: May God reward you, wise Sayf!

KHUZAA: Indeed. If each of us Arab men had himself a foreign woman we would conquer the whole of the West!

MUSTAFA: By God, I've been working on this plan all alone since I landed in England!

SAKHR [*indignantly*]: What do you mean "all alone"? Who do you think you are, the only cock in the walk? We're macho too, we have our conquests!

YAZID: Me too.

[ALL *laugh.*]

LAYTH: Don't laugh guys. This is a serious matter. We have to conquer the West socially, penetrate it by way of their women, and this is a plan no Zionism or imperialism can ever defeat so long as we all unite, act as one hand.

YAZID: No. Unity in all things but that. How on earth can we act as one hand?

SU'DUD: He means we must cooperate with each other and complement each other, brother. Every Arab stands by his brother for better or for worse.

MUSTAFA: Let's stick with the play. Today we rehearse the scene where the hero is abducted.

LUQMAN: But where is brother Fayez?

ADHAM: Nobody's seen him today.

MUSTAFA: We can't have the play without him.

SU'DUD: He may be asleep.

SAKHR [*goes to* FAYEZ's *room*]: Fayez, wake up, buddy . . . all the brothers are waiting for you.

LUQMAN: We give him the main role and precedence over all of us, and he ignores us.

SAKHR: Help everyone! Fayez has been abducted!

ALL: *What?*

TAMMAM: How do you know he's been abducted?

SAKHR: His bed's made. That means he didn't sleep here last night.

MUSTAFA: That's all? Is this proof of abduction?

SAKHR: The evidence is that my play predicted it.

MIGHWAR: We left him in his room last night. Has anyone seen him since?

[ALL *silent.*]

ADHAM: By God he's not in the habit of disappearing without telling us.

MUSTAFA: Could he have gone to the battle on his own?

TAMMAM: He ought to have waited for us.

SAYF: What matters is, how do we make sure he's safe?

YAZID: I have an idea.

ALL: Tell us.

YAZID: We wait. If he shows up tomorrow or after tomorrow, we know he's unharmed.

ADHAM: By God, this makes sense.

[*A brief silence.*]

LAYTH: Suppose he doesn't show up?

SAYF: God Protect us from your ill wishes!

KHUZAA: Think of the good, brother!

SAKHR: Are you going to wish the man ill?

LUQMAN: The bloke's right. He says "suppose." Suppose.

TAMMAM: Why doesn't he suppose something good?

MIGHWAR: Because all suppositions are equally possible. What difference does it make?

SU'DUD: Then, the Almighty will make everything right.

MUSTAFA: A prayer for the Prophet! Let's not think ill!

ALL: God's prayers upon our Prophet.

MUSTAFA: Surely, if he's not here, he has a good excuse.

ADHAM: By God, he surely has.

LAYTH: It's possible . . .

YAZID: Who knows?

MIGHWAR: Maybe and perhaps . . .

ADHAM: And if maybe . . .

SAKHR: By God, it is possible.

MUSTAFA: Wait a little . . .

ADHAM: Yes, indeed.

MUSTAFA: . . . And news will find you.

JASIR: My heart tells me all is well . . .

SAYF: Well, if God Wills . . .

KHUZAA: Well, if God Permits.

LUQMAN: God be with him. Excuse me, brothers. [*Exit, carrying a bottle.*]

ADHAM: Take me with you.

JASIR: Come on, chaps, let's go to bed.

KHUZAA: God bless.

SAYF: I'm going up.

LAYTH: And I'm going down.

ANTAR: And I am going out.

SAKHR: And I'm going in.

TAMMAM: I'm getting up.

MUSTAFA: And I'm staying put.

SU'DUD: I'm leaving.

   [*He does not budge.*]

MUSTAFA: Why don't you stay?

SU'DUD: To do what?

MUSTAFA: By God, I don't know.

SU'DUD: All right, I'm staying. [*After a brief moment, he gets up. Exit.*]

MUSTAFA [*remembering as he sees* GEORGE]: George!

GEORGE: Yes?

MUSTAFA: Tell me, have you seen Fayez since we got up yesterday?

GEORGE: Sorry, I haven't seen anybody.

MUSTAFA: Who are you trying to fool? [*He hands him a banknote.*] Take this and you'll remember.

GEORGE: Thank you. I'll tell you on condition that if anybody else gives me money I tell your secrets, okay?

MUSTAFA: No! Anything but that, George. You're under oath.

GEORGE [*returning the money*]: Rest assured, mister. George has honor. George does not tell lies. He does not snitch. He does not accept bribes. He does not stick his nose into other people's business!

Lights out.

SCENE IV

ALL *worried and preoccupied. Some sitting and others pacing the room nervously*

HIKMAT: What to do? . . . Days have gone by and not a word about Fayez. Are we going to just sit and wait?

SU'DUD: I'm depressed.

RABHA: God help his family and his people.

HIKMAT: His family are not aware of anything, sweetheart.

MUSTAFA: I dispatched a telegram to his family the following day.

GEORGE: Gentlemen, I have to call the police.

ALL: No . . . No!

SAKHR: George, don't make matters worse!

GEORGE: My dear, you yourself said that he has been abducted.

MUSTAFA: He meant "maybe," . . . maybe.

GEORGE: No, he didn't say "maybe."

MUSTAFA: Whenever we speak we mean "maybe," even if we don't say it. You just don't know Arabic.

GEORGE: But . . .

LAYTH: Fayez is our brother and we worry about him more than you do.

SAKHR: This is an internal problem between us and you have nothing to do with it.

GEORGE: Okay, anything you say. [*Exit.*]

LUQMAN: If the police come to ask us where we were that night, we'll end up being blamed for it all!

YAZID: And the Scotland Yard police, in particular, are famous for their stupidity.

ANTAR: We do not fear the police of the foreigners. We only fear our own police!

SAKHR: Yes, because the police in our countries are patriotic and they would never make any mistakes.

ADHAM: By God, you're right.

RABHA: I don't trust the English: they're prejudiced against us Arabs.

ANTAR: If any ill has befallen Fayez, God forbid, they will not avenge our honor.

SAKHR: You've hit the nail on the head.

ANTAR: It is we who must take revenge with our own hands.

SU'DUD: Then we must be patient until we investigate this matter; and we keep it our secret.

[*Exeunt some; others immerse themselves in conversation or smoking and playing backgammon. They become noisy.* ADHAM *bursts in from the main door.*]

ADHAM: Brethren! Guess what! Fayez's fiancée has arrived!

ALL: What?

ADHAM: Yeah! She's paying the cab outside.

MUSTAFA: And you let her pay? [*He reaches in his pocket with disappointment.*] Has anyone got any change?

[*No answer.* AMAL *enters. She is wearing a simple dress and carries a small suitcase.* HIKMAT *follows.*]

HIKMAT: All the brothers are Fayez's friends. . . . This is our sister Amal.

SAYF: We are honored: welcome. [*The rest greet her all together.*] Welcome, welcome.

AMAL [*standing still*]: Where is Fayez?

[ALL *silent. Some characters appear from different sides then stop expectantly.*]

RABHA: Well, make yourself comfortable first, then . . . [*Stops.*]

AMAL [*after a brief pause*]: Where is Fayez?

MUSTAFA: Didn't I send you a telegram saying . . .

AMAL [*interrupting*]: You said nothing.

HIKMAT: Fayez isn't here right now.

AMAL: Where did he go?

YAZID: We don't know.

AMAL: What do you mean you don't know? Aren't you his brothers?

ALL: Indeed, his brothers.

SU'DUD: But he's the one who has suddenly disappeared without a word.

AMAL: Disappeared how? He performed a vanishing act? He was snatched away by an eagle? Devoured by an ogre? Bewitched by demons? Lured by the sirens? How can he be lost from your midst?

[*Brief silence.*]

JASIR: I still can't believe it.

LAYTH: It's impossible.

ADHAM: Inconceivable . . . out of the question.

SAKHR: Beyond imagination, I swear.

KHUZAA: Is it real, or is it a nightmare?

ANTAR: Not one whisper . . . not one clue . . . no trace.

HIKMAT: If he had . . . if we had . . .

RABHA: I wish . . .

MUSTAFA: Prayers for our Prophet!

ALL: God's prayers upon our Prophet!

MUSTAFA: "Bear with evil and expect good."

HIKMAT: "The tide always comes in again."

SAYF: If God wills.

KHUZAA: All will be well, if God permits.

AMAL: I don't want to hear anything. I want to know where Fayez is!

[ALL *silent, heads down.*]

AMAL [*in sudden hysteria*]: Where is Fayez? Where is Fayez? . . . Where is Fayez??

Lights out.

SCENE V

[*The phone rings.* GEORGE *answers.*]

GEORGE: Yes . . . Yes . . . any one of them? Okay. [*Leaves the receiver and shouts.*] Phone call for you concerning Fayez, somebody answer the phone!

[*A few enter.*]

TAMMAM: What is it? . . . Did he say anything?

GEORGE: No.

MIGHWAR: Did he say who he was?

GEORGE: No. He said "Let me speak to one of the Arabs."

[ALL *look at each other, each expecting the other to pick up the phone.*]

KHUZAA: God Almighty, we seek Your protection.

MUSTAFA [*answering*]: Allo? This is Mustafa.

ALL [*surround him in anticipation*]: What happened?

MUSTAFA: I haven't heard anything yet! Allo. . . . Speak up please.

ALL: What's he saying?

MUSTAFA: He's saying tell these hooligans to shut up and you'll hear me!

[*They* ALL *shut up. The rest enter.*]

MUSTAFA [*concentrating*]: Unbelievable! Fayez is with you and he's safe and sound?

ALL: Praise be to God.

RABHA: Let me go tell Amal the good news! [*Exit.*]

SAYF: Congratulations, men!

TAMMAM: I knew it in my heart that he was coming back.

ADHAM: Thank God we were patient and didn't call the police.

LUQMAN [*to* MUSTAFA]: Ask him about his health, his mood.

ANTAR [*reaching for the receiver*]: Tell him to give him to me, I want to say hello.

MUSTAFA: Patience, for God's sake. He says that Fayez can come back within a week.

SU'DUD: No, tell him we want him back today.

JASIR: Yes, today, this hour, immediately and this instant.

MUSTAFA: He says okay, . . . if we first pay him a hundred thousand dollars.

ALL: *What?*

LAYTH: This is abduction and blackmail!

SAKHR: God Almighty! . . . I told you my play predicted his abduction!

ANTAR [*to* MUSTAFA]: Tell him we do not succumb to blackmail and threats.

JASIR: Tell him we'll subject him to the fiercest revenge.

MUSTAFA: He's hung up.

LAYTH: The mean scoundrel!

SAYF: The wicked coward!

KHUZAA: The contemptible thief!

LUQMAN: The despicable slime!

YAZID: May God bereave his mother.

MIGHWAR: A dollop of discipline! It's useless to curse. We must now decide what to do.

ADHAM: By God, you're right. Sit, men, let us think.

MIGHWAR: Excuse me, brothers, I am in no shape to think now. You decide then let me know. [*Exit.*]

ADHAM: Fayez is our brother, our flesh and blood. We'll pay any price. We each pay our share.

KHUZAA: Come again? And where do we get all this money?

MUSTAFA: The caller told me that we have one week to get the money and keep it ready at the hotel.

YAZID: I've got an idea. . . . Let's change hotels!

SU'DUD: And why don't we ask the police to rescue him?

SAKHR: Suppose the kidnappers kill him before he's rescued by the police?

SU'DUD: Let's try!

ANTAR: I am not paying one penny, I do not succumb to threats. But I am ready to give my whole life in ransom.

YAZID: Me too.

ALL: Me too.

KHUZAA: And may God be on our side.

SAKHR: There remains a small problem. We have to find out who is holding Fayez to be able to rescue him.

ADHAM: His fiancée's coming. We'd better keep this from her. She's faint-hearted and might not survive the shock.

SAYF [*moving away*]: It's me who's faint-hearted, and I can't watch her suffer. [*Exit.*]

ADHAM: By God, you're right. [*Exit.*]

YAZID: I'm with them. [*Exit.*]

[*Enter* AMAL *accompanied by* RABHA.]

AMAL [*joyfully*]: Have you any news? Have you really found Fayez?

RABHA: Of course . . . [*Noticing their silence.*] Why are you quiet? Tell her the news.

SU'DUD: What news?

RABHA: Didn't a man call just now saying he had Fayez?

KHUZAA: I swear by God, it never happened!

RABHA: What's with you? Are you trying to drive me crazy?

MUSTAFA: No, it's you who misunderstood. He said that concerning Fayez . . . he had . . . news of him.

AMAL: What news?

MUSTAFA: Huh? You tell her now.

SAKHR: He told us that he's away on a trip.

AMAL: Where, who with, and when does he return?

LUQMAN: No precise information.

[*Enter* HIKMAT *from main door.*]

HIKMAT: Sister Amal! . . . Good news . . . a great victory!

AMAL [*eagerly*]: Did you find Fayez? You found him?

HIKMAT: No. But I've found a bit of a trace of him.

AMAL: Had all trace of him been lost?

HIKMAT: No, listen to me. I've just been to an Indian fortune-teller!

AMAL: Fortuneteller?

HIKMAT: Yeah . . . but his words never fail! He told me Fayez will return after seven steps.

LAYTH: By God, that's correct. Seven steps mean seven days.

HIKMAT: Exactly. The Indian said the same thing: after seven days . . . or seven months, or seven years.

AMAL [*disappointed*]: And what's the use of all this?

SU'DUD: It proves that, praise be to God, he wasn't abducted or anything like that.

AMAL [*panicky*]: Did you suspect he was abducted?

RABHA: Just rumors. And now we can relax. Can't you see how pleased we are? [*She cries.*]

MUSTAFA: Sister Amal, ban all sorrow from your heart, and laugh. . . . Come on, be merry! Have you heard the latest joke? Once there was one . . . two, three . . . ! Hee hee heee! You don't like it? I can't see why. It's the latest. Okay, listen to this one: Once there was a woman . . . [*He suddenly starts choking with tears.*] who was going to cry just like you, and a man found himself about to cry like her. Excuse me. [*He rushes out.*]

[TAMMAM *starts singing and playing the lute for her.*]

LUQMAN [*beginning to draw*]: May I draw your portrait, sister Amal?

RABHA: Leave her alone, her face is all pale and emaciated right now.

TAMMAM: I want her the way she is, I want to capture this moment with her sorrowful eyes; and I'll call it "Amal Awaiting his Return."

SU'DUD: Would you accept this delicate rose from me?

[AMAL *sits completely still.*]

ANTAR: A few modest verses you inspired me to write, sister Amal. . . . Would you allow a humble, sensitive poet to read them to you?

[*Suddenly, the siren of an approaching police car.*]

ALL: Police! . . . Police! . . . At arms!

[*They move around clumsily bumping into each other. A few escape inside.*]

Lights out.

SCENE VI

GEORGE *talking to the inspector. Some* STUDENTS *watching.*

GEORGE: Meet the inspector. [*To* INSPECTOR.] These are friends of Fayez's.

SAKHR [*worriedly, on his way out*]: The rest of his colleagues are in their rooms. . . . Would you like us to call them?

GEORGE: The inspector is in no hurry.

ANTAR [*attempting to conceal his worry*]: Am I glad George called you!

GEORGE: Actually, I reported the incident two days ago, but it seems the inspector was busy investigating.

MUSTAFA: Well, inspector sir . . . have you any news?

LUQMAN: By the life of your sister, please put our minds at rest.

TAMMAM: We're so worried. We don't know left from right.

SAYF: We put our faith in you . . . and in God.

KHUZAA: Fayez is our colleague, our brother, and we are willing to help in every way.

INSPECTOR [*examining them all the while with a sly grin*]: What are they talking about?

GEORGE: Nothing, Sir.

INSPECTOR: Nothing?

GEORGE: Just words, words.

SAKHR: No, we do not speak just words; explain to him properly.

GEORGE: Then speak to him yourselves. Use your best English.

SAYF: We speak our way, and it's up to you to understand.

GEORGE: Okay, have it your way.

JASIR: Mister inspector, sir, we condemn Fayez's abduction and we hold you fully responsible.

LAYTH: We demand a just and swift investigation.

MUSTAFA: Yes, indeed. Don't you imagine you can play dumb just because he's an Arab.

ANTAR: We demand that Fayez be found and returned to us immediately.

SAKHR: Give them a reasonable ultimatum. . . . [*To* INSPECTOR.] You have twenty-four hours, no more.

ANTAR: Or else . . . we shall boycott your universities!

SAKHR: Not only that, but we'll transfer all our student exchanges to Russia!

GEORGE: The inspector can't speak to you all at the same time, and he wants to question you one by one.

SAKHR: By God, no! No good!

LAYTH: They want to separate us in order to turn us against each other; it's a conspiracy. We talk in front of all present. We are all blood brothers.

INSPECTOR: You are all blood brothers?

ALL: Yes!

INSPECTOR: Fantastic! Who is the oldest?

YAZID: None of us brothers is older than the other. We are all exactly the same!

INSPECTOR: Oh my God!

MUSTAFA: What do you mean, "Oh my God?"

LAYTH: This man is stupid . . . he thought we have the same father and mother! [*To* INSPECTOR.] We're not *real* brothers.

MUSTAFA: Mind you . . . although we're not real brothers, we are more than brothers. Yeah!

INSPECTOR: By God! I swear by the head of my dear beloved mother, by the life of my sister, you are driving me out of my mind!

LUQMAN: You can speak like an Arab!

INSPECTOR: Yes, indeed. That's why I am handling this case. Now I need some information. Who of you has last seen Fayez before his disappearance?

LAYTH: We all saw him last Saturday night and left him in his room.

INSPECTOR: And then?

LAYTH: We each went to . . . to . . .

ADHAM: To go about our business!

INSPECTOR: That night was your Feast?

SEVERAL: Yes.

INSPECTOR: And yet each of you spent it away from his brothers?

LAYTH [*annoyed*]: Are you cross-examining us?

INSPECTOR: Okay, who can describe him to me?

ALL: We all can.

MUSTAFA: He is a young man our age . . .

ALL: Acts and looks the same as all of us.

MUSTAFA: Golden brown and slim, medium height, walks tall and proud . . . uh . . . an honest man.

ALL: A man . . .

HIKMAT: A perfect man . . . respected, wise, full of hopes, full of optimism . . . the best of men!

ALL: A real man in his word, in his step, in his laughter, in his fury.

MUSTAFA: He is a prince among men, a healer of wounds.

ALL: A man.

MUSTAFA: And real men are rare.

INSPECTOR: Okay, then. Tell me about his relations with women.

ALL [*indignantly*]: Broads?!

SAYF: God protect us! He never had any relation with females!

INSPECTOR: Does he drink whisky, cognac, beer . . . ?

ALL [*indignantly*]: Liquor?! God Almighty! Never! . . . No, no . . .

INSPECTOR: Hashish?

ALL: No, no . . . God forbid!

INSPECTOR: Does he play cards?

ALL: Gambling?! God forgive us! Of course not!

INSPECTOR: Did he have any disagreement with any of you?

ALL: Disagreement? Between us? That's impossible!

INSPECTOR: Did he sometimes lose his temper . . . did he ever use bad language . . . is he ever sad . . . did he ever misunderstand anything . . . did he . . . [*Stops in despair.*]

ALL [*answering each question while mechanically shaking their heads*]: No, no, no, . . .

INSPECTOR: Allow me one last question.

MUSTAFA: Your wish is our command, your excellency.

INSPECTOR: Does he eat and drink and walk in the marketplace like us? Does he sleep and wake up and sometimes feel tired—God forbid—like us?

[*They put their heads together and whisper, conferring, shaking and nodding their heads.*]

YAZID: What is it, exactly, you are implying?

INSPECTOR: Ladies and gentlemen . . . only now can I tell you where your friend has gone.

ACT ONE

SEVERAL [*anxiously*]: Where, where, where?

INSPECTOR [*sarcastically, pointing up*]: He has risen to the heavens! He's obviously spread his wings and flown. You can write to him at his address in Paradise. . . . Anyone like him must be an angel, not a man!

JASIR: We refuse to accept any mockery of our brother.

INSPECTOR: Listen carefully. Saturday night, there was a robbery at the Pleasure Palace. Investigations indicate that most of the patrons were Arabs, and maybe Fayez was among them.

ALL [*quickly*]: No!

KHUZAA: Fayez does not frequent brothels.

INSPECTOR: Were any of you there that night?

ALL: No!

INSPECTOR: Then how do you know Fayez was not at the Palace?

ANTAR: Because we know Fayez as well as we know our own souls.

LAYTH: And how did your policemen know that the patrons were Arabs, when they were all wearing masks?

INSPECTOR: Maybe Arabs don't recognize each other. But with the means at our disposal, we can recognize them even if they're disguised.

YAZID: What would you gain by besmirching Fayez's image?

INSPECTOR: On the contrary, I have his interests at heart. He might have been attacked during the robbery.

SAKHR: You mean that the robbers are the kidnappers?

INSPECTOR: That is a possibility. We have received anonymous letters giving their description, but that does not constitute evidence. We must have an eyewitness to identify them.

[ALL *are quiet, exchanging confused glances.*]

INSPECTOR: Speak up and help me rescue him. Tell the truth even if it exposes some of his weaknesses.

YAZID [*glances at* AMAL]: We do not talk about a brother in his absence.

INSPECTOR: Then you don't really want him back. All you want is to preserve his good name.

MUSTAFA: And what is a human being but a good name? It's worth the whole world, your excellency.

INSPECTOR: I see my business here is finished . . . [*He starts to go.*]

AMAL: No, wait. You are the police and his case is your responsibility.

INSPECTOR: What you need is a magician or a fortuneteller to solve the mystery of his disappearance.

AMAL: You mean abduction. Fayez was abducted, and they might be torturing him right now.

INSPECTOR: You are his fiancée?

AMAL: Yes.

INSPECTOR: I understand your feelings. But you can't issue judgments without evidence.

AMAL: Fayez's case is clear; and that evening in particular he had been attacked by some foreigners.

INSPECTOR: Why didn't you speak up? Who were these foreigners?

RABHA: He didn't recognize them. They just roughed him up in the street.

INSPECTOR: What nationality were they? Arabs? Indians? Africans?

RABHA: No, foreigners . . . English people!

INSPECTOR: I'm sorry, miss, but *you* are the foreigners.

RABHA: No, I'm no foreigner. . . . I'm an Arab, so how can I be a foreigner?

INSPECTOR: Because you are here in England. . . . That makes you the stranger.

HIKMAT: By God, nothing is stranger than your own behavior. By your honor, tell me: are you proud that a guest in your country is humiliated and beaten up and called the worst of names because he is an Arab?

INSPECTOR: I understand. . . . Could your friend Fayez have run away?

JASIR: Run away? Why?

INSPECTOR: He was embarrassed when he was humiliated and failed to retaliate.

AMAL: No, Fayez is no weakling; he's no coward.

TAMMAM: No Arab takes humiliation in silence, or fails to take revenge.

INSPECTOR [*smiling coolly*]: Words . . . words.

SAKHR: No, not words; this is the truth.

ADHAM: You in the West don't know the Arabs and don't appreciate their valor.

LAYTH: Yes. The Zionist lobby has presented you with a fake picture of the Arabs and you've swallowed it.

INSPECTOR: Where is this picture, in books?

RABHA: In books and newspapers and television as well.

MUSTAFA: You should know . . . whoever sprays us Arabs with water we spray with blood!

INSPECTOR [*writing furiously in a small notebook*]: " . . . we spray with blood."

ANTAR: We never forget our revenge; and death to our enemies!

INSPECTOR: " . . . never forget our revenge." [*To them.*] Now the crime is clear.

LUQMAN: Now you are convinced that there was a crime?

INSPECTOR: Yes. Last Saturday night, a bomb exploded in a bookshop, and based on your statements I charge your colleague Fayez with arson as an act of revenge. That bookshop sells anti-Arab books.

AMAL: These are all lies! Slander! Fayez couldn't do such a thing!

ADHAM: You don't know the Arabs and you don't appreciate their passion for peace!

INSPECTOR: You are now altering your words.

KHUZAA: You've lured us into saying words we didn't mean.

LUQMAN: But this bookshop sells books attacking everything, not just Arabs; so why do you accuse Fayez alone?

INSPECTOR: And who would think of burning books . . . if not an Arab?

AMAL [*leaping toward him in rage*]: You're biased against us . . . you're a racist . . . a Zionist . . . a bigot!

[HIKMAT *and* RABHA *hold her back.*]

JASIR: We're reporting you to the authorities!

INSPECTOR: And I am asking each one of you to give, in writing, details of where you spent Saturday evening and what you did, and to send those statements to the investigative authorities within forty-eight hours. Good night, gentlemen. [*He tips his hat and leaves.*]

[*A moment of silence. They exchange looks, trying to read each others' minds.*]

KHUZAA: I wonder . . . where lies the truth?

LUQMAN: Incomprehensible . . . incomprehensible.

SAKHR: Was Fayez that mysterious?

TAMMAM: Or is it us who never understood him?

MIGHWAR: Or never tried to understand him.

LAYTH: Since when do we try to understand each other?

YAZID: Or even understand ourselves?

MUSTAFA: Just imagine if he actually did set fire to the bookshop . . .

ANTAR: Without telling us or consulting us? Then he must bear the consequences alone.

JASIR: Or, otherwise . . . he spent the night at the Pleasure Palace.

SAYF: By God, if any ill befell him there . . . he deserves it all!

ADHAM: By God, you're right. Morals before everything.

[*They start to exit in different directions. Enter a* WOMAN *walking suggestively.*]

WOMAN: Hello.

ALL [*stopping to stare*]: Hello.

WOMAN: How are you?

ALL: Fine, thank you.

WOMAN: I'm Eve.

ALL: I'm Adam

EVE [*laughing*]: Ohhh, lovely!

ALL: It's you that's lovely!

EVE: You are sweet, brothers.

ALL: Do you know us?

EVE: Of course, darlings.

ALL: Welcome, welcome . . . a million greetings!

EVE: I've missed you . . . I've missed you . . . I've missed you!

ALL: And we've missed you more.

LUQMAN: But, you do know us?

EVE: One by one, honey.

LUQMAN: You must be my relative!

EVE: And I know all your secrets . . . your frolics, in detail!

[*They look confused and nervous.*]

EVE [*extracting a cigarette*]: Someone give me a light!

ALL: I'll light it with my fingers!

KHUZAA: Come on, tell us who you are.

EVE: I'm Fayez's friend. His *girlfriend!*

ALL [*surprised*]: *What?*

Curtains. End of Act One

Act Two

SCENE I

M. ANNOUNCER: Dear viewers . . .

F. ANNOUNCER: Excuse us . . .

M. ANNOUNCER: We have to admit that Fayez's colleagues have lost interest in his case.

F. ANNOUNCER: Only temporarily . . .

M. ANNOUNCER: Due to their suspicions concerning his morals and their confusion in the face of the police accusations.

F. ANNOUNCER: Or rather, because they are awaiting the investigation results.

M. ANNOUNCER: Whatever the reason, each is preoccupied with his own life.

F. ANNOUNCER: And the sequences we are about to show are scenes from their personal lives.

M. ANNOUNCER: Kindly don't ask us how we acquired them.

F. ANNOUNCER: Although we have our colleague the cameraman to thank . . .

M. ANNOUNCER: And our colleague the producer.

Lights out.

In the hotel. Sequences of shots taken at different times.

[HIKMAT *comes forward under the spotlight, followed by* MUSTAFA.]

MUSTAFA: How are you, Hikmat?

HIKMAT: What are you doing speaking to me now?

MUSTAFA: Why not? You're my compatriot!

HIKMAT: Can you tell me then—what is the purpose of our talk?

MUSTAFA: I'm sorry I asked how you were!

HIKMAT: After "How are you?" you're going to say "Let's go for a stroll along the Thames"!

MUSTAFA: Exactly . . . anything wrong with that?

HIKMAT: Can you tell me then—what is the purpose of this stroll?

MUSTAFA: All this because I said "How are you?" Thank God I didn't say "Hello, love!" . . . You would have told me to apologize or something!

HIKMAT: Scoot! Go find yourself a foreign woman to ooze your charm on.

MUSTAFA: And why not? Is there no way to please you? [*Exit.*]

HIKMAT: I hope you return home married to a foreigner, and it turns out she had Aids!

[*Enter* SAYF.]

HIKMAT [*immediately*]: Yes, brother Sayf, you've been staring at me all day. . . . Can you tell me—what is the purpose of this ogling?

SAYF: No, nothing!

HIKMAT: What do you mean "nothing"? Well. Can you tell me then: where is the job contract you promised me?

SAYF: It's ready. Why the rush? I'll give it to you after graduation.

HIKMAT: Here I am: I'm dressed modestly and I've stopped talking to any of the men in our group. Any other conditions?

SAYF: God forgive me! That was a piece of advice from one man to his sister, nothing else. But I wish you'd speak like us.

HIKMAT [*angry*]: How do I speak?

SAYF: Oh . . . words pour out of your mouth like sweet nectar!

HIKMAT: Can you tell me then—what is the purpose of this talk?

SAYF: Sneak into my room: I'll follow you there.

HIKMAT: You . . . miserable wretch!

SAYF [*coolly*]: By God, you've passed! I was testing your morals! From this instant, you don't need to worry about salaries or family responsibilities, or even worry about your Ph.D. . . . Happy?

HIKMAT: Forget my worries over expenses and work? All right! . . . But drop my Ph.D. when I've only got a few months to go? . . . I'd be an ass!

SAYF: Look, I have American girls throwing themselves at my feet, and you want to challenge me as an equal? Your master's degree is sufficient for you; leave the Ph.D. to me.

HIKMAT [*faking coyness*]: You impose your conditions and humiliate me to agree to marry me?

SAYF: Forgive me, God Almighty! Who ever mentioned marriage?

HIKMAT: Why are you being so tyrannical then? You want to keep me in the house and cover me from head to toe . . . by what right? You think I'm a slave you can buy with your money?

SAYF: Try to understand me. . . . Before I marry you I need a permit from my government.

HIKMAT: What's the permit for?

SAYF: Because you're a foreigner!

HIKMAT: Oh, yeah? Really? You'll marry me in heaven, chuck!

SAYF: I heard that! And who may Chuck be? Speak up. You'd better speak . . .

[HIKMAT *begins to speak but is cut off.*]

SAYF: Not one word! I'm glad I figured you out now! [*Quickly walks away.*]

[*Enter* MUSTAFA *and* MARGARET.]

MUSTAFA: Margaret, do you love me?

MARGARET: Very much.

MUSTAFA: Say it in Arabic.

MARGARET: Okay . . . habibi.

MUSTAFA: Ohhh . . . super! Yes, my sweetheart?

MARGARET: Can you tell me where our love is going?

MUSTAFA: I wish I hadn't asked her to speak Arabic! What's with you, Margaret? . . . Shame on you! You're supposed to be modern!

MARGARET: I must worry about the future, Mustafa.

MUSTAFA [*agitated*]: But I can't leave my homeland. Not for all the treasures in the world!

MARGARET: No problem . . . I'll go home with you.

MUSTAFA: You love me that much? We have the highest pollution and noise and overpopulation factors in the world.

That's besides the food and housing shortages, and tons of misery!

MARGARET: I'd live with you on bread and water.

MUSTAFA: Still, I'm afraid we might not be happy. See, our values are different.

MARGARET: Why darling? I value justice, I value good. And you value tyranny? You value evil?

MUSTAFA: Of course not!

MARGARET: Okay. I value truthfulness, I value tolerance. And you value dishonesty? You value bigotry?

MUSTAFA: What is this leading us to? Honestly, Margaret, my family will tell me it's a disgrace, it's a sin, it's immoral . . . they won't let me.

MARGARET: Won't let you what?

MUSTAFA: Marry you, of course.

MARGARET: Who ever mentioned marriage?

MUSTAFA: What?

MARGARET: All I want is your word that we'll remain friends all our lives.

MUSTAFA: Are you serious? You won't regret not getting married?

MARGARET: If marriage in your country is a disgrace.

MUSTAFA: Done!

MARGARET: But we must take an oath, Mustafa.

[*Exeunt.* KHUZAA *comes in from the street with a* GIRL *carrying an umbrella.*]

KHUZAA: You are very beautiful.

GIRL: Thank you.

KHUZAA: You are like a rocket!

GIRL: What?

KHUZAA: You are like a bomb!

GIRL: Oh no! You are a fool!

KHUZAA: Praise the Lord! You Western girls have a weird temper . . . I'm wooing you! I'm telling you you are a rocket, you are a bomb! Don't you understand your own language? Okay, I'll speak to you in the universal tongue. Give me one! [*Pouts, asking for a kiss.*]

[*Enter* RABHA. *She is shocked to see* KHUZAA.]

GIRL: Can you?

KHUZAA: Can I? . . . You bet I can . . . nothing can stop me!

RABHA [*attacking him and screaming*]: What a scandal, you miserable . . . !

KHUZAA: But you don't understand . . . I am on a national mission!

RABHA: You don't say!

GIRL: What's the matter?

KHUZAA: You, leave now. [*To* RABHA.] Listen to me, Rabha. The chaps took the decision to degrade foreign women as a means of taking revenge on the whole of the West! This is an obligation. And if I don't fulfill it I'll be dragging my people into disgrace! Would it please you if they said we have no men?!

RABHA: They couldn't find anybody else to carry out this filthy mission?

KHUZAA: I'm not alone, we're all executing this plan.

RABHA: Well, excuse me just a moment. [*She moves to leave.*]

KHUZAA [*anxiously*]: Where are you going?

RABHA: To execute the Arab women's part of the plan. [*Exit.*]

KHUZAA: You wretched . . . !

[*Quick lights out, then on. A number of students and* GEORGE *surround* EVE *and sing to her.*]

ALL: Happy birthday to you!

EVE: Oh, thank you. [*She dances with each in turn, to a waltz.*]

SAYF [*embarrassed, gives her a present*]: Allow me to offer you a modest gift.

EVE [*coolly*]: A solitaire ring?

SAYF: With a three-carat stone.

EVE: Thank you! [*She hands it to* GEORGE.]

SAYF: Could we . . . maybe . . . sometime . . . go somewhere together for tea?

EVE: Later . . . later.

SU'DUD [*whispering and reaching into his pocket*]: I got you something.

EVE [*curious*]: What?

SU'DUD [*looks around then draws out a rose*]: Here! [*Whispering.*] I'll be in my room tonight . . . [*Imperatively.*] Don't you be late!

YAZID [*drawing his dagger*]: I offer you the dagger of my ancestors.

LUQMAN: I knocked on your door many times last night to give you your present.

EVE: Naughty boy!

LUQMAN: Next time, if you don't open up, I'll kick the door down!

MUSTAFA: Come on, Eve! . . . You made me wait two hours for you yesterday on the embankment. The Thames is blowing ice!

EVE: Sorry, darling, I was busy.

MUSTAFA: It's your loss. I was going to offer you two bottles of the best beer. This is the seventh time you've missed the chance of your life. . . . So, when do we meet tonight?

EVE: Just like yesterday, darling.

MUSTAFA: Fine, honey. [*To himself.*] Just like yesterday? I'm being taken for a ride!

LAYTH: Allow me to offer my dearest possession! My copy of *Revolutionary Unity between Fundamentalism and Contemporaneity.*

EVE: I don't understand.

LAYTH: I want to be alone with you to explain it.

EVE: With pleasure.

[*The music ends.* ALL *move toward* EVE *and talk to her.*]

EVE: Thank you everybody. Excuse me, five minutes, I'll be back. [*Exit, followed by* GEORGE *laden with presents.*]

[AMAL *appears and all are quiet.*]

LUQMAN [*after a moment of silence*]: Welcome, Amal. Welcome! welcome! . . . Come in. Excuse me!

AMAL: Wait . . . why are you avoiding me? Why do you clam up the moment you see my face? You can't bear to listen to me or speak to me or speak about him!

KHUZAA: God Forbid! . . . But such are the ways of life. We all have our problems.

AMAL: And how will Fayez ever be found if you're all so selfish?

ADHAM: If we knew where he'd vanished to, we could help him.

AMAL: So now you call his plight "vanishing"?

RABHA: Bear with us. We sleep and rise in perplexity.

AMAL: This is called defeat!

SAKHR: We didn't fail in our duty. We are no cowards. We haven't forgotten. We're thinking, looking for a plan.

AMAL: This is called defeat!

ANTAR: How? When we have not even started the battle?

AMAL: Defeat happens here in the *brain*. Then, the *will* declines and the *determination* disintegrates. Armies are deployed and trumpets are blown and soldiers are led to the battlefields of destruction with the sole purpose of boasting *successes!*

MUSTAFA: Brothers, this is too much. . . . Somebody tell her the truth.

[*A moment of silence as they exchange glances.*]

HIKMAT: Sister Amal . . . Fayez has another lover.

[AMAL *stares blankly at her.*]

HIKMAT: I know it's a shock. But the truth is painful.

AMAL: What is the meaning of these words?

HIKMAT: They mean you must forget him. He dumped you and got himself a foreigner. He's not even worth one of your tears.

AMAL: No! . . . No, it's all lies.

RABHA: How can you be sure it's lies?

AMAL: How do babies recognize their mothers? How do birds sense earthquakes before they happen? I know, because the truth dwells in the heart and lies stay outside. None of you has known him. You are not his brothers. You were never his friends.

TAMMAM: Satisfied?

AMAL: You ask me how I know? Here is his letter . . . his last letter to me. [*Reads.*] My darling, my friend, source of all my blessings. I kiss your hands and the hem of your dress and I pray to God that He may protect you and watch over you. . . . I shall be back by your side very soon. Wait for me at the northern window in your pink dress.... Don't forget ... I'm coming back, I won't be late.... I miss the sun bathing our roof in warmth, and the poultry in the courtyard. I miss the fields, the lofty palms ... I miss my aunts and the little ones ... and spicy food.... You asked me about embroidering the sheets ... do them in green ... I think that would be best ... or do them in all colors. I will soon be back.... I send you love, my precious Amal, my dream. Love to all the family and friends and everybody in the house. P.S. Don't forget to water the plants. Forever faithful, Fayez.

[ALL *silent with their heads down.*]

ADHAM: Definitely, sister Amal, the man who wrote this letter could never be disloyal; there is no way he would be a coward.

HIKMAT: Come, Amal. From this day on we'll never leave you alone.

[*Exeunt* RABHA, HIKMAT, *and* AMAL.]

JASIR: We've let time slip by. The one-week ultimatum is almost over.

KHUZAA: We're not to blame ... it's the days that go too fast!

MIGHWAR: The problem is, if he shows up now the police will arrest him.

MUSTAFA: Let him show up first, then God will take care of everything.

[EVE *comes out of the room.*]

EVE: I have the solution.

LUQMAN: How do you know what we're talking about?

EVE: A little bird told me. The point is that I've got what you need to rescue Fayez and get him back safely.

JASIR: Tell us.

EVE: I know a man ... on condition you pay him.

KHUZAA: We'll pay.

EVE: One hundred and twenty thousand dollars.

SAYF: What? This is more than the ransom money!

EVE: But Fayez will return with dignity, and you'll get the credit for saving him. What do you say?

ALL: We say no!

EVE: Remember this: If Fayez is dead tomorrow or the day after, you have murdered him.

Lights out.

SCENE II

In the studio.

F. ANNOUNCER: We continue to follow up on the case of the Arab student . . .

M. ANNOUNCER: Fayez . . . ,

F. ANNOUNCER: A case which has aroused public opinion.

M. ANNOUNCER: The British press claims that he is the terrorist responsible for the bookshop fire.

F. ANNOUNCER: And, as usual, the papers were filled with indiscriminate anti-Arab articles.

M. ANNOUNCER: The reaction from Arab lands comes from the other end of the spectrum.

F. ANNOUNCER: Immediately following the publication of the news, all Arab organizations and unions cabled their support for Fayez.

M. ANNOUNCER: There were demonstrations all over London and other British cities in his support.

F. ANNOUNCER: And his colleagues were inundated with donations in support of his cause.

M. ANNOUNCER: In consequence, his colleagues decided to hold an extraordinary meeting to study his case.

F. ANNOUNCER: We'll keep you informed in a detailed report . . .

M. ANNOUNCER: Prepared and presented by . . .

F. ANNOUNCER: Sadiqa Salih . . .

M. ANNOUNCER: . . . and Amin Falih.

DIRECTOR: Stop! That's good, but you must speak about Fayez with more fervor.

M. ANNOUNCER: You too want to glorify him, as they do?

DIRECTOR: Yes, he is a hero because he refused to be humiliated. He proved to be a man of honor.

M. ANNOUNCER: Shame on you, you believe what the British say about him? They want to portray him as a criminal . . .

DIRECTOR: Would you rather have me believe that he was at the brothel disgracing us all?

M. ANNOUNCER: Not at all. This would incriminate them and prove that Fayez is being victimized.

DIRECTOR: You deny us the honor of having a hero to show off to our children?

M. ANNOUNCER: A hero "book burner"?

DIRECTOR: These are books full of lies, calling for our massacre.

M. ANNOUNCER: Answer bullets with bullets, and answer books with books. Sadiqa, say something, let's hear your opinion.

F. ANNOUNCER: What can I say? He wants to say that Fayez burned the books because this would make him a hero; you want to say he was at the brothel to make him a victim. Guys, these are opinions. No one has asked for the truth.

DIRECTOR: How would we know it? Only God knows the truth.

CAMERAMAN: Actually, I have no tolerance for books. But for me it's out of the question that anyone, no matter how oppressed, would set fire to a bookshop. He must be an ignoramus, and certainly well paid by somebody or other. I'm going shopping in Oxford Street. Anybody join me?
Lights out.
Hotel bar. Semicircular bar facing the audience. Voices shouting outside.

VOICES: Our hands in yours . . . our power with yours . . . power and might! We give our pledge . . . we give our oath . . . we hail you . . . fiercely! With our souls . . . with our blood . . . we avenge you, Fayez!
[ANNOUNCERS *appear.*]

F. ANNOUNCER: Dear viewers,

M. ANNOUNCER: In a few moments, the critical events of the vital meeting called by the Arab brothers will begin.

F. ANNOUNCER: As there is no suitable conference room in the hotel . . .

M. ANNOUNCER: They are using the only place spacious enough to accommodate them.

F. ANNOUNCER: They've just filed in.

[*We see the* STUDENTS *walking with serious determination, carrying thick files with the legend "Fayez's Case" in their hands or under their arms.*]

M. ANNOUNCER [*to* SAKHR]: Tell us your impressions of . . .

SAKHR: Enough talk . . . it's time for vital ideological action.

F. ANNOUNCER: Your comments on . . .

SAYF: No comment, no comment.

M. ANNOUNCER: Your expectations regarding . . .

ANTAR [*his hand raised giving the victory sign*]: This, or else . . .

F. ANNOUNCER: Your opinion about . . .

KHUZAA: Success, God willing.

M. ANNOUNCER: The framework within which . . .

LAYTH: No retreat . . . no negotiations . . . no surrender.

F. ANNOUNCER: How about the contributions you've been receiving?

ADHAM: We gratefully accept contributions, but we refuse to allow anyone else to take charge of the defense in our friend's cause because it is our right and nobody else's.

M. ANNOUNCER: A word concerning . . .

SU'DUD: I want to say hello to my family and relatives: I'll send you the medicine as soon as possible.

JASIR: Please, let us work in peace.

[ANNOUNCERS *withdraw.* ALL *sit on stools. Each noisily sips from his glass then inhales from his cigarette and exhales slowly in deep thought.* AMAL *appears on one side and looks at each of them.*]

MUSTAFA [*rises and raises his hand*]: Brothers, the oath . . .

ALL [*rise quickly*]: God be my witness. . . . From this instant . . . we may not rejoice . . . we may not sing or play . . . we may not love . . . until our brother Fayez returns . . . and the mystery is resolved. We swear to act together, as one hand, . . . scorning all our differences . . . with no recourse to our governments or embassies. We seek help from God alone. And by the might of our arms and our intelligence . . . we swear before you, sister, . . . that we shall have no life . . . until Fayez returns . . . *in full glory!*

AMAL: God be with you, men! [*Exit.*]

[*Brief silence, then they all speak together.*]

MIGHWAR: A dollop of discipline to start with, brothers . . .

ALL: Go ahead, go ahead . . .

MIGHWAR: I remind you of our everlasting agreement: no discussion of politics or religion or ancestry or sex or football . . . and so on!

ANTAR: I request the inclusion of that statement in the minutes.

SAKHR: I request the exclusion of that statement from the minutes.

TAMMAM: There are no minutes!

YAZID: Then I'm in charge of the minutes.

MUSTAFA [*tapping the table*]: Brethren, silence please. The meeting is open. [*Gradual silence.*] In the Name of God the Compassionate, the Merciful . . . Fellow Arabs . . .

ANTAR: Are we to shut up so that you can speak on your own?!

MIGHWAR [*raising his hand*]: A dollop of discipline!

MUSTAFA: Do you all want to speak at the same time?

TAMMAM: We all have equal right to speak.

MIGHWAR: A dollop of discipline!

SU'DUD: This is mayhem!

MUSTAFA: Everyone will have the chance to speak, in turn.

SAKHR: How did you come to be heading this meeting? I don't see any stripes on your arm!

JASIR: I'd like to make it clear, for your information, that I will not allow anyone whatsoever to dictate to me . . .

MIGHWAR: A dollop of discipline, please.

MUSTAFA: I don't mean to impose myself, but somebody has to run this meeting.

SAYF: Very well . . . I'm ready to run the session. Sit down. . . . Fellow Arabs! . . .

ANTAR: I am also prepared to direct this session. . . . Brethren! . . .

MIGHWAR: Fellows! A dollop of discipline!

MUSTAFA: Wait, let's hear him out. Speak up, brother Mighwar.

MIGHWAR: Brothers, we are supposed to be . . .

SAYF [*to* MUSTAFA]: By what right do you give him the floor?

KHUZAA: Indeed. . . . This means you're running this meeting.

MUSTAFA: All he's asking for is a dollop of discipline.

SAYF: Whatever . . . I demand a dollop of discipline as well!

MUSTAFA: Do you know what "a dollop of discipline" really means?

JASIR: Oh no . . . there's no end to this.

KHUZAA [*calmly*]: Don't fret, brother.

JASIR: Don't stifle my freedom! I have every right to fret and object and attack . . . and also withdraw!

KHUZAA [*agitated*]: Withdraw then, brother. Don't threaten us . . . we don't take to blackmail.

JASIR: All right . . . I am *out*, for *real*. [*He rises.*]

YAZID [*rising*]: So am I!

MUSTAFA: A prayer for our Prophet! . . .

ALL: God's prayers upon our Prophet! . . .

[GEORGE *enters. Fills each glass with mineral water then exits.*]

SAKHR: In the Name of God the Compassionate the Merciful . . . the meeting begins.

ANTAR: Over my dead body!

MUSTAFA: What's your problem? Let's do it the Western way. Let's use democracy.

SAYF: What did you say?!

MUSTAFA: We need a teenie weenie injection.

SAYF: By God, brother, no . . . "Give him an inch and he'll take a mile!"

MUSTAFA: Has anyone got another solution?!

MIGHWAR: I've got one, a dollop of discipline.

MUSTAFA: Later, not now! Let's have nominations. . . . If you think you're worthy of chairing this meeting, please raise your hand.

[ALL *raise their hands.*]

MUSTAFA: This is no good. Some of us have to stand aside so that we have people to vote.

SAYF: Are you willing to stand aside?

MUSTAFA: Of course not!

SAYF: Then shut up!

JASIR: I object! This is nonsense! And I don't associate myself with such trivialities.

YAZID: I'm with him!

LUQMAN: Are you giving up, brother?

JASIR: No, but I'm out . . .

YAZID: I go along with him.

MUSTAFA: Wait, don't be rash. . . . We can make something great out of this situation.

ANTAR: Leave him alone. One down, all down. We do not succumb to threats or ultimatums!

JASIR: I'm withdrawing but I'm not leaving. [*He turns his back to all.*]

SAYF: Keep your mouth shut, then.

JASIR [*looking around*]: I'm not keeping quiet! [*Turns his back again.*]

YAZID: Neither am I!

[*He takes up* JASIR*'s posture.*]

SAKHR: Brother, instead of quitting and turning your back on us, withdraw your nomination and vote for me.

JASIR: And I shall not withdraw!

SAKHR: Face us then.

JASIR: And I won't face you.

YAZID: Neither will I.

MUSTAFA: Brothers, a prayer for our Prophet.

ALL: God's prayers upon our Prophet!

LUQMAN: Brethren, if it will solve the problem . . . I withdraw my nomination.

MUSTAFA: Please, a round of applause for our colleague Luqman. [ALL *applaud.*]

SAKHR: Now that we have a voter, the elections meet their legal requirements.

MIGHWAR: A dollop of discipline.

MUSTAFA: Patience. . . . The floor now goes to the distinguished voter, and we must all abide by his judgment.

LUQMAN: Brothers . . .

MIGHWAR: A dollop of discipline, if you please.

LUQMAN: I cannot give you the floor. I'm simply a voter. Only the chairman I choose has such authority.

ALL [*applauding loudly*]: Praise be to God!

MUSTAFA: Now, our hero, our leader . . . which of us do you elect?

LUQMAN: I ask you to present your manifestos to enable me to opt for the best, if any.

[ALL *talk at the same time.*]

LUQMAN: No. This is chaos, and I do not tolerate chaos. None of you may utter one word without my permission. Understood?

JASIR: I object! The voter here is a minority and we cannot allow the minority to dictate to the majority.

SAKHR: Jasir, you are attacking him because he won't vote for you.

LUQMAN: I didn't ask you to speak for me. Shut your mouth.

SAKHR: Me too?

LUQMAN: Yes, I am sole owner of all votes here. . . . I alone am the people and no one else has the right to open his mouth!

SU'DUD: This is called minority dictatorship!

SAYF: This is evidence of decaying democracy!

LAYTH: Brothers . . . for the sake of preserving our solidarity, I announce the withdrawal of my nomination.

MUSTAFA: And I salute your bravery!

SAYF: Of course, you want us all to withdraw so that you win by default.

LUQMAN: I've ordered you to be quiet once, don't force me to give you notice of dismissal.

LAYTH: Note that now you are no longer the only voter and that I enjoy equal rights. . . . That means you may not dismiss anybody without me saying so! You dismiss one, I dismiss three!

MUSTAFA: This way the votes will be equal and we'll have no winner.

MIGHWAR: A dollop of discipline!

ADHAM: In consequence of the present situation, we must halt the electoral process and discuss matters.

KHUZAA: We motion the abolishment of the foreign Western invention called democracy.

SAYF: We motion the return to authentic Arab traditional laws.

MUSTAFA: I fully support you, and according to our traditions the oldest is chairman and I am the oldest.

SOME: Sit down! . . . Shut up! . . . Demagogue! . . . Populist! . . . Elitist!

SAYF: By God, no, brother . . . the leader is oldest in wisdom not by age or status.

ADHAM: By God, you're right . . .

[ALL *applaud.*]

SAYF: And as I am the wisest and the most farsighted and the most religious . . .

VOICES: Sit down! . . . Shut up! . . . Enough!

MIGHWAR: Please, I've been requesting a dollop of discipline for more than an hour.

MUSTAFA: We have no chairman to give you the floor. Just speak.

MIGHWAR: Brethren . . .

MUSTAFA [*suddenly*]: That's it, I've got it!

SOME: What?

MUSTAFA: I've found a compromise. We draw straws. This way, we'll all have equal status and we let luck decide who will be leader.

SAYF: Don't say luck, say God's will. Those in favor of brother Mustafa's motion raise their hand.

MUSTAFA [*quickly, before anyone reacts*]: Agreed! It's unanimous!

SAKHR: Let's move now to the central question: who do we elect to organize the draw?

ANTAR: Anyone. Is this a problem?

JASIR: Don't make a problem out of nothing.

LAYTH: These are formalities . . .

SAKHR: Then, I organize the draw.

ANTAR: No, anyone but you!

SAKHR: Oh God!

JASIR: I'm fed up, restless, and disgusted. I'm withdrawing permanently!

SAKHR: Sit down!

JASIR: I will not!

TAMMAM: Be reasonable!

JASIR: I will not be reasonable!

LAYTH: This is treason and conspiracy against our united front!

ANTAR: You are all agents of the enemy!

ADHAM: This is chauvinistic populism!

SAYF: This is heresy!

KHUZAA: This is apostasy!

ANTAR: Passive elitism, reactionism!

SAYF: Communists!

YAZID: Imperialists!

ANTAR: Shut up, you Arab! [*He hits* KHUZAA *with a plate.*]

KHUZAA: See, everybody?

ANTAR: Get out of my way! . . . Leave him to me!

SAKHR: If you let them beat each other up, I'll beat you all up!
[*Enter* GEORGE.]

GEORGE: I don't allow punch-ups in here. This is a respectable place.

[*Temporary silence.* GEORGE *goes to replenish* KHUZAA's *glass from the bottle of water.*]

KHUZAA [*covering the glass with his hand*]: That's enough.

SAYF: God Save us from damned Satan!

KHUZAA: Indeed. It all comes from the devil. The jinn control us and alter our souls.

ANTAR: By God, no. I am mightier than fifty jinns! [*Hiccups.*]
[*They* ALL *look drunk and start hiccuping.*]

MIGHWAR [*begging for attention*]: Brothers . . . hic! . . . we are gathered here . . .

MUSTAFA: You're boring us . . . hic! . . . What do you want?

MIGHWAR: We must first define the problem which . . . hic . . . is bringing us here together.

ANTAR: No, it is not important . . . hic . . . to define the problem, but why not define it anyway?

MUSTAFA: Great idea . . . hic . . . what problem does your excellency suggest we discuss?

MIGHWAR: I have no problems at all!

MUSTAFA: Then who . . . hic . . . has a problem?

ANTAR: Why look at me? I have no problems . . . hic . . . look at yourselves!

KHUZAA: May God prevent all problems, buddy!

SU'DUD [*suddenly wakes up and yawns*]: God is all-merciful.

YAZID: If there are no problems, why did you call for a meeting then?

SU'DUD: Could it be something to do with brother Fayez?

SAKHR: Yes! It's brother Fayez's case. . . . Shame on you, did you forget?

LAYTH: The contributions we've received will cover the ransom. But if we pay, the whole world will ridicule us.

TAMMAM: And if we refuse, they'll kill Fayez and we'll suffer the guilt of failure.

LUQMAN: Thus, we are forced to accept Eve's offer.

JASIR: Surrender and pay the ransom?

ANTAR: No, just a deposit, not the whole sum. We give it to Eve and she delivers it to the gang through her friend, and he asks them to give us a few more days.

ADHAM: By God, you're right. This will give us some time to think and the case stays hot.

MUSTAFA: Agreed? [*No answer.*] Silent majority!

SAKHR and ANTAR: No . . . we object to these decrees unless they are top secret.

JASIR: I object. That's not enough. We must issue other, public decrees.

SU'DUD: Tell us what to do, man, and let's get it over with.

JASIR: We issue Communiqué Number One, a harsh communiqué from the United Arab Students to the whole of free Europe: We fiercely denounce what happened to our friend Fayez. Please return him to us as soon as possible. And if you do this again, we'll be very angry with you, and we'll invoke God's wrath upon you!

DIRECTOR: Stop!

CAMERAMAN: Yes sir!

[*Actors freeze.*]

DIRECTOR: Rewind the tape and add some background music.

CAMERAMAN: All right . . . all right. Don't fret.

[*The last few sentences are repeated to the sound of dance music.*]

DIRECTOR [*angry*]: Stop! . . . What is this mess?

CAMERAMAN: Don't you want cheerful music to drown this wretched atmosphere?

DIRECTOR: Some fiery music, an anthem . . . a stirring song!

CAMERAMAN: Oh, like the music we use when we win a football match!? Yes sir, just don't fret.

[*Replays the last scene to a military march.*]

JASIR: . . . a harsh communiqué from the United Arab Students to the whole of free Europe.

[*Lights out—*ANNOUNCERS *appear.*]

M. ANNOUNCER: But this communiqué had no impact worth mentioning.

F. ANNOUNCER: And days went by with no news.

M. ANNOUNCER: Fayez's friends were deluged with letters and telegrams.

F. ANNOUNCER: And this time, they were messages of denunciation . . .

M. ANNOUNCER: We can summarize in one question:

F. ANNOUNCER: "What have you done for Fayez?"

M. ANNOUNCER: We put this question to them.

F. ANNOUNCER: And here is their reply.

Scene III

The hotel. A few STUDENTS. MUSTAFA *sitting to one side. On the other side, others are nervously pacing to and fro.* LAYTH *enters gasping for breath.*

LUQMAN [*anxiously*]: What happened?

ADHAM: Let him catch his breath.

LAYTH: I went to the enemy's lair. I sneaked around and stopped where my heart told me to look, I peeked . . .

SAKHR: Through the keyhole.

LAYTH: Through the keyhole. Do you know who I saw?

ADHAM: Who? Our abducted brother?

LAYTH: Yes, in the flesh!

LUQMAN: Thank God, so he's still alive!

YAZID: Heroes do not perish.

LAYTH: But I found him shackled in chains, with torture scars on his back: whip lashes!

ANTAR: We are not succumbing to threats and blackmail and we are not paying ransoms!

YAZID: If they have touched a hair on his head, I swear I'll kill ten of them! I'll cut them down with my sword!

TAMMAM: Ten dead will not quench my thirst. I'll throw a bomb at them and burn them all!

LAYTH: Let's go rescue him tomorrow.

ANTAR [*spreads a map*]: Look at this map. Here is the enemy camp. This is our plan.

MUSTAFA [*stands up*]: Stop! . . . You were great . . . the best!

[ANNOUNCERS *suddenly appear, the* CAMERAMAN *behind them.*]

MUSTAFA [*seeing the camera*]: But there are some comments . . .

M. ANNOUNCER: Excuse us, sorry for the interruption.

MUSTAFA [*feigning surprise*]: Wow! We're on television! [*Coyly.*] You should have told us!

[ALL *greet the* ANNOUNCERS.]

M. ANNOUNCER: May we have two minutes of your time?

MUSTAFA: With great pleasure.

F. ANNOUNCER: Explain to our viewers what we've just seen.

MUSTAFA: This is a scene from our play "Woe Ye Arabs." We intend to stage it soon for the whole Arab community in England and Europe.

F. ANNOUNCER: And what is this play about?

MUSTAFA: I don't know. My colleague Sakhr is the playwright. He can answer your questions.

SAKHR: Actually, it's a serious play with a serious message. It represents, symbolically, the plight of our brother Fayez. It's the least we can do for him.

M. ANNOUNCER: Allow me. Don't you feel that the subject matter is presented in a somewhat exaggerated fashion?

MUSTAFA: I don't know. Mister Jasir is our critic, he can answer you.

JASIR: On the contrary, I find that the play is lacking in revolutionary fervor.

F. ANNOUNCER: Don't you think that the element of truth is vital to the impact of the play on the audience?

JASIR: No, by God. I believe that acting is an opportunity to exaggerate and go to extremes to teach the audience and explain to them; because our audience, unlike foreign audiences, understands.

F. ANNOUNCER: Would you show our viewers another exerpt?

MUSTAFA: With great pleasure. Everybody get ready.

[*Enter* EVE.]

EVE: My friends . . . your deadline has expired and they'll kill your friend.

RABHA [*whispering*]: Sshhhh! . . . We have guests.

EVE: Okay, you handle the gang. I have no time for you.

SAKHR: We have some of the ransom ready.

EVE: Is this a fridge you're paying for in installments? Are you buying your friend Fayez?

ANTAR: We put faith in your friend, he will convince them. . . . Brother Adham, hand her the briefcase.

ADHAM [*handing her the case*]: But you tell them to treat him humanely!

EVE [*on her way out*]: Why are you whispering . . . we're not stealing anything!

M. ANNOUNCER [*applauding*]: Bravo, great . . . very professional!

HIKMAT: That wasn't acting! The tragedy is—it's real!

MUSTAFA: She means this scene of the tragedy . . . but, of course, good triumphs, you'll see.

[ANNOUNCERS *and* CAMERAMAN *retreat to a far corner.*]

MUSTAFA: Rehearsal! Let's do the last scene again!

JASIR: We want warmth. Layth, wear the blood makeup. You don't have blood? Use ketchup.

[AMAL *enters looking haggard.* ALL *take their positions to start acting.*]

LUQMAN: What happened?

ADHAM: Let him catch his breath.

LAYTH: I went to the enemy's lair. I sneaked around and stopped where my heart told me to look; I peeked through the keyhole and do you know who I saw?

ADHAM: Who? Our abducted brother?

AMAL [*sotto voce*]: Fayez . . .

LAYTH: Yes, in the flesh!

LUQMAN: Thank God, so he's still alive!

YAZID: Heroes do not perish.

LAYTH: But I found him shackled in chains with torture scars on his back: whip lashes!

AMAL [*suddenly screams*]: Bastards! [*To* LAYTH.] Didn't you try to save him?

LAYTH: No, I was afraid the enemy might see me.

AMAL: Coward!

HIKMAT: Sister, they're acting.

LAYTH: Let's go rescue him tomorrow.

AMAL: Lies! Don't you dare. . . . Take me to him . . . take me to Fayez!

SAKHR: It's not Fayez, sister, we are talking about the hero.

AMAL: And who is that?

MUSTAFA: Actually, he's a symbol, an imaginary character in the play.

AMAL: You're pretending, you're lying to me, you don't want me to know where he is. [*She holds on to* LAYTH.] Where did you see him? Speak!

RABHA: Sister, they don't know where he is.

AMAL: No, they know everything but they're cowards. [*With determination.*] But I'm not leaving him alone . . . I'll find my way to him! [*Heads for the door.*]

HIKMAT: Amal, where are you going?

AMAL: I'll follow the birds, they'll lead me. . . . I'll follow the roar of thunder in the bosom of the heavens, I'll follow the wail of storms in space . . . I'll follow the flames of fire in the woods . . . I'll follow the trails of blood and the stench of treason and the moans of humanity everywhere. They will lead me to him.

Lights out.

SCENE IV

The studio.

F. ANNOUNCER: In the latest development in Fayez's case . . .

M. ANNOUNCER: Professor Wisdom, renowned orientalist, . . .

F. ANNOUNCER: Invited Fayez's Arab and European fellow students . . .

M. ANNOUNCER: To an open debate.

F. ANNOUNCER: And as Professor Wisdom is renowned for his great intelligence and fairness . . .

M. ANNOUNCER: We went to meet him, and this is what he said: [PROF. WISDOM *appears, seated.*]

F. ANNOUNCER: Good night, Professor.

PROF. WISDOM: Excuse me, it's "Good evening."

F. ANNOUNCER: Sorry . . . hello. Tell us, what is the purpose of this debate?

PROF. WISDOM: All evil stems from ignorance. Dialogue is an important tool in recognizing the opinions of any opposing party; a means to overcome mutual suspicions and doubts.

F. ANNOUNCER: But we want to familiarize ourselves with your personal attitude concerning Fayez's case.

PROF. WISDOM: All I know is that he is innocent of the charge of the bookshop fire, because a man is innocent until proven guilty.

F. ANNOUNCER: What do you think of the Arab point of view that he is a victim, abducted by fanatical Europeans?

PROF. WISDOM: It is possible. Fanaticism and racism plague the whole world; the Arab world in particular!

DIRECTOR: Stop! . . . Is this what you call neutral?

PROF. WISDOM: Do I have to preach your point of view to be considered neutral?

M. ANNOUNCER: What would you say if I told you that two days ago, English speakers in Hyde Park openly demanded the obliteration of all Arabs?

PROF. WISDOM: Don't be so touchy!

CAMERAMAN: They're demanding our annihilation, pop, and you say "don't be touchy"? By God, I'm filming you in black and white!

PROF. WISDOM: I mean, these speakers are mentally disturbed. However, you too, even though you're not English, have equal right to speak and call for the execution of the Queen herself!

CAMERAMAN: Hell! . . . They'll put you in prison, Doc!

F. ANNOUNCER: What's the use of democracy if it permits sick people to express destructive thoughts?

PROF. WISDOM: Its advantage is that it also allows constructive thoughts, no matter how daring, to be expressed without fear; thus improving society. As for sick people, no one will listen to them.

F. ANNOUNCER: Oh, we forgot to ask you. Are you a supporter of Zionism?

PROF. WISDOM: No, I have no sympathy for Zionism whatsoever . . .

F. ANNOUNCER [interjecting]: Thank God!

PROF. WISDOM: Just as I have no sympathy for Arab nationalism. We shouldn't become fanatical over anything but justice and peace.

M. ANNOUNCER: Let's go back to the crux of the debate.

PROF. WISDOM: The European students agreed to participate, but the Arab students are hesitant. So, why are you Arabs afraid of dialogue?

M. ANNOUNCER: The problem is that you try to impose dialogue on us. For example, look what happened to Fayez.

PROF. WISDOM: Note that your rejection of dialogue with anyone means that you consider him an enemy. And lack of dialogue inevitably leads to violence.

M. ANNOUNCER: It is the West which uses violence against us. We have never attacked them.

PROF. WISDOM [*smiling*]: True. But it doesn't necessarily mean that you're angels. Perhaps the reason is that you haven't got the power to dare to attack the West!

DIRECTOR [*into the earphone*]: I swear this man is prejudiced and he hates us like hell! Ask him the question we talked about.

M. ANNOUNCER: Yes sir. [*To* PROF. WISDOM.] Some say that orientalists like yourself study the Arab heritage in order to serve imperialistic purposes and intelligence agencies. What do you think?

PROF. WISDOM [*coolly*]: Everything is possible! But don't forget that thousands of Arabs study European societies and have equal opportunity. As for myself, if I was working for intelligence agencies I wouldn't tell you! Hee hee!

F. ANNOUNCER: Professor Wisdom . . . may we ask you a personal question?

PROF. WISDOM: Go ahead.

M. ANNOUNCER: If you yourself don't harbor the seed of prejudice, would you allow your daughter to marry an Arab?

PROF. WISDOM: My daughter is free to do as she wishes with her life.

F. ANNOUNCER: Understood. But we are asking you about your emotions. Would you be sincerely happy for her?

PROF. WISDOM [*thinking*]: All right . . . an Arab is a human being like us and . . .

M. ANNOUNCER [*interrupting sarcastically*]: Thank you for this valuable recognition!

PROF. WISDOM: Sorry, that's not what I meant. I didn't mean it the way you took it . . .

F. ANNOUNCER [*interrupting*]: No matter. . . . Would you be happy if your daughter married an Arab?

PROF. WISDOM: I dislike hypothetical questions immensely.

M. ANNOUNCER: You're evading the question.

PROF. WISDOM [*annoyed*]: No, but you're asking me about something I haven't experienced.

M. ANNOUNCER: What would you say if I told you that your daughter actually intends to marry an Arab?

PROF. WISDOM [*artificial laugh*]: You're joking, no doubt.

F. ANNOUNCER: Dear viewers . . . we are pleased to have with us in the studio . . . Miss Margaret Wisdom! Come in!

[*Enter* MARGARET.]

MARGARET: Good evening, Daddy.

PROF. WISDOM [*stunned*]: Oh my God! Is it true what I hear?

MARGARET: Yes, Daddy. I've fallen in love with a young Arab man, and he's teaching me to speak Arabic.

PROF. WISDOM: It's true you speak Arabic like an Arab!

M. ANNOUNCER: Now, Professor, have you experienced your true feelings?

PROF. WISDOM: Fine. I'm surprised, no more. I shall be happy when I know that the young man is suitable for her, regardless of his nationality.

MARGARET: I could ask him over for tea to meet you, Daddy.

PROF. WISDOM: I would prefer to meet him under different circumstances. Would he agree to participate in the debate?

MARGARET: Of course, Daddy. He's a wonderful man.

PROF. WISDOM: Fine. It would be a good opportunity to evaluate his character.

M. ANNOUNCER: We are certain that all Arab students are up to the challenge.

PROF. WISDOM: Dear sir, I'm not talking about challenges. It's a question of dialogue . . . simply a dialogue between two parties. . . . Is that difficult?

Lights out.

SCENE V

The hotel.

F. ANNOUNCER: Dear viewers . . .

M. ANNOUNCER: We are with the Arab students on the eve of the awaited debate, . . .

F. ANNOUNCER: Examining their feelings and their preparations.

KHUZAA: This is a good opportunity to clear our image in the eyes of the West, which still imagines us riding camels in the streets.

LUQMAN: More importantly, it's an opportunity to change their view of Fayez's case so that they take it seriously.

[MUSTAFA *enters with* MARGARET.]

MUSTAFA: Greetings everybody. I've got hot news!

DIRECTOR: Stop!

MUSTAFA: Sorry. But Margaret was in the European students' camp and she brings you their secrets.

HIKMAT: Camp? Are we starting a war?

MUSTAFA: Yes, they formed a camp and they're getting ready for us. Tell them, Maggy.

MARGARET: First, they're preparing a general statement about progress in the West.

HIKMAT: Easy. We prepare a statement about progress in the Arab world.

YAZID: Our embassy has no information at all!

LUQMAN: Ours does . . . but God knows how much of it is true.

MUSTAFA: Ours is prepared, but the staff are not there. They're out enjoying themselves or shopping or changing money.

MARGARET: Anything you need to know about any Arab country is in the public library.

SAKHR: I warn you: if we use one line from those books we'll be revealing our national secrets.

MARGARET: How? It's all in print, everyone has access to this information.

LUQMAN: We would've had no problems if the officials in our countries did any reading.

SAKHR: What did you say?

CAMERAMAN [*winking*]: He says officials have no time to read. God help them . . .

DIRECTOR: Don't worry. We're not filming yet.

M. ANNOUNCER: Go on Margaret, what else are they doing?

MARGARET: Training. Training for the dialogue.

KHUZAA: Training to speak? How? Are they sharpening their tongues?

MARGARET: Yes. They select a few to act as Arabs and they speak with your logic!

YAZID: What good does that do?

F. ANNOUNCER: They're preparing their minds for what we're going to say instead of being taken by surprise. That way they're ready with their replies.

TAMMAM: And those who play the Arabs, can they imitate us?

MARGARET: Yes, they were very good! And we laughed and clapped, because their arguments were fantastic!

KHUZAA: Why don't you pass these arguments on to us? Let's get it over with, instead of all this thinking and headaches!

MARGARET: Certainly, you can defend yourselves much better.

ADHAM: Okay, you're a foreigner, and you're aware of your weaknesses. Tell us some . . .

MARGARET: My friends . . . I'm not against my country. I love you because I love Mustafa and I want everybody to love everybody else!

MUSTAFA: Don't waste time. Let's do the same. . . . Who'll play the foreigners?

[*No reply.*]

MUSTAFA: Nobody? You then, Luqman.

LUQMAN: What do you mean? Am I less of an Arab than any of you? I swear, by God, I'm not playing with you ever again! [*Exit.*]

MUSTAFA: What's this child's play? Are we playing catch?

SAYF: So you act grownup and play the foreigner.

MUSTAFA: What? Why me?

MARGARET [*to herself*]: Even you, Mustafa?

HIKMAT: I tell you what . . . Mr. Amin decides.

M. ANNOUNCER: Easy. Eenie, meenie, mynie, mo . . . you and you and you.

[*Points at* RABHA *and* JASIR *and* YAZID.]

ALL THREE [*annoyed*]: We have no choice!

DIRECTOR [*to* CAMERAMAN]: Ready?

CAMERAMAN: Ready . . . go.

RABHA: Your main weakness, you Arabs, is that you hang on to traditions and abide by morals all the time.

JASIR: You Arabs are fanatics. Yes indeed, fanatical with regard to nobility and valor, even with strangers, and this is bad!

YAZID: You Arabs are impulsive. In any confrontation you plunge into danger with no fear of death!

[MARGARET *laughs loudly.*]

F. ANNOUNCER: Are these weaknesses, or evidence of pride? You've shamed us in front of foreigners!

ANTAR: Why don't *you* just play these roles, and let us get on with it!

BOTH ANNOUNCERS [*exchanging glances*]: No objection.

M. ANNOUNCER: But beware. We're foreigners, we speak freely.

TAMMAM: This is acting, why should anybody mind?

MIGHWAR: A dollop of discipline, brothers. Since we're getting serious, we have to exclude Margaret. She shouldn't be made aware of our weaknesses.

MUSTAFA: But she's on our side. She gave us the idea.

HIKMAT: Nonetheless, foreigners are forbidden to witness our dirty linen!

LAYTH: Besides, how do you know? She may be a spy, buddy!

MUSTAFA: Shame on you, men . . . I trust her with my own neck!

MARGARET: It's all right Mustafa . . . I understand how they feel.

[*To* ALL.] I appreciate your feelings. . . . See you tomorrow.

MIGHWAR: Excuse me, friends, I have no tolerance for arguments. [*Exit.*]

[*Exit* MARGARET. ANNOUNCERS *appear, wearing Western hats.*]

F. ANNOUNCER: We're ready!

SAKHR: Question: How come the police, up till now, are in cahoots with the kidnappers?

F. ANNOUNCER: Question: If you have any doubts concerning police integrity, why are you studying Law in our country?

SAKHR: True, you've put down modern laws and constitutions, but you're the first to trample justice.

M. ANNOUNCER: You emigrate and come to live in our midst by the millions!

RABHA: If you have emancipation and civilization, why do you have homosexuality and theft and murder and even rape?

F. ANNOUNCER: Well, look who's talking! You, the epitome of purity and wisdom. You, the immaculate; your closets are overflowing with rattling skeletons. . . . The difference between you and us is that we don't shy from the truth!

MUSTAFA: If your people are happy and free, why does Europe in particular have the highest suicide rate in the world?

F. ANNOUNCER: If you have any morals or conscience, why are people perishing of starvation in your countries?

JASIR: Thanks to you: your imperialism has exploited us day after day.

M. ANNOUNCER: This is an argument you use to purge your souls, to wipe out your failures and helplessness.

ANTAR: Question! . . . If the missing student was a European, wouldn't Britain have been up in arms by now?

M. ANNOUNCER: If a thousand people vanished in an Arab country, would anyone dare open his mouth?

ALL: What?

CAMERAMAN: Hell!

ADHAM: We're just starting; are we already getting into a jam?

DIRECTOR: No hitting below the belt, Amin!

M. ANNOUNCER [sarcastically]: Darling, you either let us do what we have to do, or forget it!

KHUZAA: I can't listen to such impertinent talk. I'm leaving!

YAZID: So am I.

[Exeunt KHUZAA and YAZID.]

F. ANNOUNCER: Hooray! The tough guys withdraw at the first hitch!

M. ANNOUNCER: Nobody has yet answered my question. Who holds whom to account when you're making your own people homeless, holding them hostage, and torturing them?

TAMMAM: What's that got to do with you? . . . We're free among ourselves!

M. ANNOUNCER: You mean free to enslave each other. But we decided, a long time ago, to free the human race from slavery and to protect an individual's rights, regardless of race or color.

HIKMAT: Lies! We're the last thing you think about! You've formed Green parties fighting for trees and associations for the protection of animals, and you build schools and hotels and psychiatric clinics for dogs. And then you give us loans with interest and you dump your surplus mountains of food into the sea without offering any to the destitute in needy countries!

M. ANNOUNCER: But we give you everything! The 'yummy' you eat, we give you. The booze you drink, we give you.

SU'DUD: I haven't tasted any of this!

M. ANNOUNCER: You study in our countries, you bank your money in our countries, and you cavort in our countries. When you're ill, you have treatment in our countries and you die in our countries!

F. ANNOUNCER: You got everything "ready-made." You're a burden to the civilization we have built with our knowledge and our will power and our independence.

LAYTH: We've paid for everything dearly, with our sweat and our strength and our blood, sucked by your imperialism. And sometimes we've even paid with our honor and independence.

M. ANNOUNCER: Did you hope to guzzle everything for free? By God, that's just great! Do we give you planes and factories and machinery and channel your water and electricity and sewage and telephone lines just for the sake of your gorgeous eyes? Maybe we ought to give you pocket money! Are you a distant branch of the family, or did we bear you and abandon you?

RABHA: You're heathens! You'll go to Hell!

F. ANNOUNCER: You're mad! You want to establish Heaven and Hell on earth. You turn the now into Armageddon, today into the Day of Judgment; then five or six of you pass judgment on the whole of humanity before God does!

MUSTAFA: All indications point to the fact that your civilization is on the way out. Within a few years you'll be saying "What happened?"

M. ANNOUNCER: These are the fantasies of fools arguing in coffee houses. Had we no humane principles, we would have flattened you with an atomic bomb.

JASIR: What are we waiting for? More degradation? I object and I protest and I quit! [*He does not leave.*]

F. ANNOUNCER: You're a lazy, backward bunch!

RABHA: You're heretical lunatics!

M. ANNOUNCER: Dumb, naive ignoramuses . . . ignorami?!

HIKMAT: Cold-blooded, cruel . . .

F. ANNOUNCER: Bloody, lowly, clumsy . . .

SU'DUD: Heathen, sinful, effeminate . . .

M. ANNOUNCER: Fanatical puritans . . .

ADHAM: Degenerate racists . . .

M. ANNOUNCER: Stupid, illiterate . . .

TAMMAM: Pretentious, conceited . . .

F. ANNOUNCER: Dictatorial . . .

ANTAR: Crooks, jesters, swindlers . . .

M. ANNOUNCER: We are reason.

MUSTAFA: We are justice.

F. ANNOUNCER: *We* are justice.

HIKMAT: We are morality.

M. ANNOUNCER: We are the present.

RABHA: We are the past and, God Willing, we are the future.

F. ANNOUNCER: Ha ha . . . really? How come? You want to relive your glories just like that? With no effort? A piece of cake!

M. ANNOUNCER: Why not? They have a wild imagination. May Shamhurish the king of all demons bring back their dusty glory, because their excellencies are too lazy to reach out and retrieve it for themselves!

ADHAM: Enough sarcasm and insolence! By God, this is wrong!

M. ANNOUNCER: What were your countries like before our boats and ships landed there? Did your currency lead the world and did we deflate it? Did you discover oil and extract it and process it and export it on camelback, then did we raid your caravans and rob you?

LAYTH: You dare defend imperialism?!

M. ANNOUNCER: You were one Arab nation and we came as a thorn between lovers? We instigated the rift between Syria and Egypt, Egypt and Sudan, North Sudan and South Sudan?

South Yemen and North Yemen? We started the wars in the Western Sahara and in the Arabian Gulf? The only thing your rulers agreed upon was the subjugation of your own people!

ANTAR: No, this is definitely more than I can take.

M. ANNOUNCER: Have we disturbed an old sore?

F. ANNOUNCER: Amin, that's enough. Don't provoke them.

M. ANNOUNCER: Are you afraid of Mommy and Daddy? Daddy the chief or the emir, and Mommy the government! The powers we bow to?

SAKHR: Enough! Even foreigners don't utter such ugly, despicable words!

M. ANNOUNCER: You haven't heard anything yet! You'll get much more in the debate!

RABHA: Woe, woe, woe . . . shame on you! What's happened to you? You're denouncing your own race and forgetting you are Arabs! May God rid us of you, a thousand times over! [Exit.]

F. ANNOUNCER: Didn't you ask us to pretend?

HIKMAT: Did you have to take it so seriously?

M. ANNOUNCER: Is acting a joke?

MUSTAFA: Of course! Actually, our government calls it entertainment, and theaters fall under the censorship of the morality police.

SU'DUD: Nightclubs. Maaan!

SAYF: Do you believe me now when I tell you that acting is sinful and that discussion always ends in disaster?

SAKHR: How can you speak like them, unless you've been poisoned?

M. ANNOUNCER: You're the ones with poisoned minds! You suffer from brain paralysis and mental anemia!

ANTAR [angrily]: You are still arguing? We said no more acting!

M. ANNOUNCER: I'm not acting now. I'm speaking my mind!

MUSTAFA: Is that so? You've overstepped the bounds of decency!

F. ANNOUNCER: Amin, what are you saying?

M. ANNOUNCER: I was pretending to hold the European argument. But after what I've heard, I believe they're in the right!

SAKHR: Tear off your mask, you double agent!

M. ANNOUNCER: That's what you do best . . . swear, wag your tongues, babble . . .

CAMERAMAN [*pushing one of them out of the way of the camera*]: Get out the way, I can't work!

LAYTH: Zionist! Imperialist! You're betraying our cause, you agent . . .

F. ANNOUNCER: That's enough, Amin. [*Holds on to him.*]

CAMERAMAN [*to* LAYTH]: I didn't manage to get that on film. Please, by the life of your father: repeat what you just said.

LAYTH: Zionist! Imperialist! You're betraying our cause, you agent . . .

M. ANNOUNCER [*to* F. ANNOUNCER]: Let me go! . . . I don't allow anyone to defy me, or pretend to be more patriotic than I am!

ANTAR: Are you going to shut up or shall I kill you this minute? [*Draws a gun.*]

F. ANNOUNCER: Help!

HIKMAT: Oh my God! Help!

CAMERAMAN [*drops the camera*]: Kill? Who do you think you are, buddy?

DIRECTOR: Sadiqa, take him out of here!

M. ANNOUNCER [*exiting with* F. ANNOUNCER]: Me a traitor? . . . You hypocritical animals! Beasts!

ANTAR: Let me teach him a lesson, this Europeanized bastard!

CAMERAMAN: Listen here, behave yourselves and watch what you say!

MUSTAFA [*pushing the others out of the way*]: Make way, just leave him to me! [*Grabs* CAMERAMAN's *neck.*]

HIKMAT [*squeezing between them*]: Are you both out of your minds?

CAMERAMAN [*to* MUSTAFA]: I'm letting you go, just because there are ladies around.

MUSTAFA: And this film you've just taken, it's not to be aired.

DIRECTOR: Don't worry . . . I swear by my honor it won't be aired and no one will see it.

CAMERAMAN: No way. I'm airing this sequence. I swear by all that God has bestowed on me, I *will* show it and disgrace you all!

LAYTH: You? You should worry about your own disgrace at the Pleasure Palace!

DIRECTOR: The Pleasure Palace?

CAMERAMAN [*sudden intuition*]: By God, you've given yourselves away!

DIRECTOR: What are you talking about?

CAMERAMAN: Shall I say, or will you?

ADHAM: By God, you're right. What's going on, brothers, let's praise God!

ALL: Praise be to God, there is no God but God!

SAKHR: We're all Arabs. We're all blood brothers. It's shameful to fight among ourselves!

ANTAR: Give me your head. [*Kisses the* CAMERAMAN's *forehead.*]

DIRECTOR: I don't understand a thing!

Lights out.

The studio.

F. ANNOUNCER: Amin, you have to admit that you went too far.

M. ANNOUNCER: *You* have to admit that you got scared.

F. ANNOUNCER: Don't forget that we all belong to the same people.

M. ANNOUNCER: That's exactly why I shouldn't deceive them. . . . No nation has the least hope of developing as long as it deceives itself.

F. ANNOUNCER: But you've actually been brainwashed! Too much reading of foreign books and magazines.

M. ANNOUNCER: Are you accusing me of being guilty of reading? Indeed, I'd need to be illiterate to accept my people's logic!

F. ANNOUNCER: You mustn't allow yourself to be affected by everything you read.

M. ANNOUNCER: I see. March down the middle for a while, don't make waves. Form some parties . . . but not for real. A free press . . . only in part. A constitution . . . you're joking! Free, open thought . . . not too open, might catch a cold! Think for a few seconds then go back to sleep . . . because this is taboo, that's a sin, and this is a shame. Oh God!

F. ANNOUNCER: Yes! Because there are taboos and there are sins and there are rules!

M. ANNOUNCER: Naturally: the taboos and sins and rules Mommy drew up, because we're all infants in the cradle— no, infants might grow up one day—yeah, because we're all mentally retarded!

F. ANNOUNCER: You defy society on your own . . . I've got limits I can't cross!

M. ANNOUNCER: So . . . you dream of being head announcer?

F. ANNOUNCER: Not one more word!

M. ANNOUNCER: You too want to gag me?

F. ANNOUNCER [*calmly*]: No, Amin. But I don't want your engagement ring anymore. [*She removes it from her finger and puts it on the nearest surface.*]

M. ANNOUNCER [*astounded, then wailing*]: Sadiqa . . . !!!

F. ANNOUNCER: We're not good for each other anymore. Go find yourself a civilized foreign woman.

M. ANNOUNCER: I can't marry a foreigner! I can't bear living abroad!

F. ANNOUNCER: I know. But you'll never be able to turn me into a foreigner and Egypt will never be England! [*Exit.*]

[CAMERAMAN *rushes in.*]

CAMERAMAN: Go after her, man! Don't let her go to bed upset!

M. ANNOUNCER [*stubbornly*]: I don't allow anyone to treat me like a child! [*Shouts in her direction.*] I deserve to be weaned . . . Foreigners are no better than we are . . . .

CAMERAMAN: I think you're both dumb! . . . You'll lose each other over nonsense!

M. ANNOUNCER: Nonsense?

CAMERAMAN: Of course. Forget Europe and forget America and all that rubbish . . . Egypt is the Mother of the World, brother! [*Exit.*]

[DIRECTOR *in the control room speaking into the intercom.*]

DIRECTOR: Amin, you're exhausted . . . go get some sleep so you can work tomorrow.

M. ANNOUNCER: I can't tell my viewers anything that doesn't emanate from the depths of my being. Go find yourself another parrot.

DIRECTOR: And what about the debate? Who's going to present it with Sadiqa?

M. ANNOUNCER: We've already lost the debate before it's even started. . . . We've lost the case before it's been examined.

DIRECTOR [*desperately*]: You are hopeless.

[*Fades out of the room with fading light.*]

M. ANNOUNCER [*into the microphone*]: Five, four, three, two, one. Your honors, the Judges . . . your honors, the Counselors of the First World . . . The peoples of the Arab nation from the Third World beseech you and appeal to you to justly repeal your verdict sentencing us to death and to replace it with a verdict of hard labor for twenty-five generations. And may God's mercy be our only comfort!

Lights out.

SCENE VI

A scene in Hyde Park. Three small step ladders symmetrically arranged center stage. A fence in the background.

F. ANNOUNCER: Dear viewers . . .

CAMERAMAN: From Speakers' Corner in Hyde Park in London, this program is presented to you by . . .

F. ANNOUNCER: Sadiqa Salih . . .

CAMERAMAN: . . . and Lutfi Fahmi.

[DIRECTOR *appears, filming.*]

F. ANNOUNCER: The long-awaited debate will begin in a few moments . . .

CAMERAMAN: Between the Arab team and the foreign team. As we all know, this debate is not easy for us, as it's taking place in their land in the midst of their supporters! But I can see a number of Arab supporters as well!

DIRECTOR: Sadiqa, don't let him speak alone!

F. ANNOUNCER: We are now awaiting the arrival of both teams to start the match . . . [*Correcting herself.*] . . . sorry! I mean the debate!

[*The* ARAB STUDENTS *enter and stand behind the steps on the right.*]

CAMERAMAN: I can see now the Arab team entering the field. Our team today is made up of Mustafa and Sakhr and Antar and Mighwar and Jasir. The substitutes are Adham and Layth.

[*The* EUROPEAN STUDENTS *enter and stand behind the steps to the left.*]

CAMERAMAN: The European team is represented by Jean-Paul and Sam and François and Ehrhard and Papakov and Margaret. . . . Actually, Margaret is a surprise today as she joined the team at the last minute! If you ask me: "Do we have any hope of winning, Captain?" My reply is: "Of course. Because this is a dialogue, and we're very good at word games. We're the best at tongue-wagging! True, we never achieve anything we talk about . . . but tomorrow is another day . . . plenty of time to come!"

DIRECTOR: What the hell are you doing?

[PROF. WISDOM *enters and stands behind the central step ladder.*]

CAMERAMAN: Don't fret. I can see Professor Wisdom coming down. He's signaling the start of the debate . . . and here we go!

PROF. WISDOM: Dear students . . . I am confident that the human race will soon see the day when artificial barriers between nations will collapse, these barriers which create suspicions, misunderstandings, and enmities. The day when all peoples will merge into one single civilization governed by love and peace. I admit that the major responsibility for making this a reality lies with the people of the West, who have an obligation to offer help to their brethren in the East. . . . We hope that this debate will be one step on that road and an opportunity for all of us to become acquainted with each others' opinions, calmly and objectively. Let's begin with the Arab party. First speaker, please take the floor.

[SAKHR *takes a step forward but they grab his clothes and pull him back. They confer—like contestants in a quiz show—whispering, heads close together, in obvious agitation.* SAKHR *goes forward again.*]

SAKHR: We'd prefer if they started, so that we know what they have to say before we reply.

PROF. WISDOM: No objection.

[*He signals to the Europeans. One comes forward and starts to speak.*]

ANTAR: We object!

STUDENT: What?

PROF. WISDOM: But he hasn't said anything yet!

ANTAR: We object to what he is about to say!

PROF. WISDOM: It's your right, but let him speak first.

JASIR: What use would our reply be then? We simply refuse to listen!

PROF. WISDOM: You could block your ears. [*Signals to the student to begin.*] Please, go on.

STUDENT: Ladies and Gentlemen . . .

JASIR [*to* PROF. WISDOM]: You're taking their side?

MUSTAFA: Naturally . . . they're your people, how could you be against them?

PROF. WISDOM: Quiet please, or else I'll have to cancel the debate.

MIGHWAR: We would like to draw our colleagues' attention to the rule that they are not, under any circumstances, to embark on topics concerning politics or religion or ancestry or sex or history or nationalism; they are also categorically forbidden to attack, directly or indirectly, or even symbolically, any great Arab figure, past or present. Other than that, we are prepared to participate with open hearts and minds.

[ALL *applaud.*]

MARGARET: We came here to have a dialogue, not to be muzzled!

MUSTAFA: And we offer you, from our side, the promise not to mention any sensitive topic which might cause any grievance to any of you. So, Margaret, don't create trouble!

MARGARET: There are no "sensitive topics" from our point of view. . . . We're not afraid of dialogue and we insist that it be carried out with total freedom of speech!

JASIR: And we refuse any dialogue without guidelines and restrictions. And we announce our withdrawal in protest against this chaos!

PROF. WISDOM: Of course, you're free to do as you like; but I have to express my disappointment at this conclusion.

[*His voice is drowned by whistles and jeers from the European side. Exit* PROF. WISDOM *in despair.*]

JASIR: Let's go, men!

[*Both parties move to the bottom of the stage, except* MUSTAFA *and* MARGARET *who meet in the center.*]

MARGARET: Hard luck, Mustafa.

MUSTAFA: You were pretending to be a friend of the Arabs?

MARGARET: Did you forget that it was your friends who sent me away and didn't want us to keep our friendship?

MUSTAFA: So what if they're suspicious of you? You're a foreigner! Does it mean you have to stand against me and insult me?

MARGARET: I did not stand against you, Mustafa; this was purely a discussion . . .

MUSTAFA: Our women do not dare discuss with their men!

MARGARET: It seems that your men also do not dare discuss anything!

MUSTAFA: Don't denigrate my people . . . I'm warning you!

MARGARET: Daddy told me that our marriage in your country is neither a sin nor a disgrace . . . Were you lying to me?

MUSTAFA: No, I swear I . . .

MARGARET [*interrupting heatedly*]: Shut up! You swear—that means you're lying. Now I'm sure! [*She cries.*] When you were courting me and telling me jokes and tickling me to make me laugh, you were playing with me!

MUSTAFA: True, it all started as a joke, but it ended in disaster! [*Hesitates.*] I mean, it ended seriously! I realized I loved you. I love you and I can't live without you.

MARGARET: On your terms, darling, and I don't accept your terms.

MUSTAFA: Why, Margaret? Remember?: "I value truth, I value justice and tolerance. And you value deceit and tyranny?"

MARGARET: It's no good. It's over.

[*A* YOUNG ENGLISHMAN *comes to her side and stares at* MUSTAFA. HIKMAT *comes to* MUSTAFA'*s side and looks at* MARGARET *with hatred.*

MUSTAFA *and* HIKMAT *move to the bottom of the stage; so do* MARGARET *and the* YOUNG MAN. *Groups exchange disdainful looks, then start to laugh and jeer. They show off their strengths and skills provocatively, which ends in chaotic fist fights to the tune of appropriate music. Gradual lights out and the sound of a police siren.*]

Lights out.

SCENE VII

The hotel. STUDENTS *file in silent and exhausted. Some go to their rooms.*

ANTAR: What happened?

SAKHR: You're asking me? All of a sudden we were in a wild fight, and I thought *Great!*

MUSTAFA: The foreigners started it.

YAZID: By God, had we not been forced to run, I would have shown them no mercy! But we couldn't stay after we heard the police siren.

ADHAM: I took my revenge and much more. I punched to my heart's content! [*Sits down and moans.*]

ANTAR [*regretfully*]: What a shame—some of those badly hurt were English friends of mine.

SAKHR: How strange. You never mentioned you had any English friends!

KHUZAA [*angrily pointing to his swollen eye*]: You feel sorry for them and feel no regret for your blunder with me? [*To the others.*] He left the foreigners and hysterically beat the hell out of *me!*

ANTAR: I did not mean to beat you up. I was trying to terrify the foreigners and make them surrender without any bloodshed.

SAYF: Shall I tell you the truth? You shouldn't have allowed them the opportunity to lure you into a fight. We're here to learn, not to fight.

MUSTAFA: Oh really?

KHUZAA: Yes. They could have us blacklisted and ban us from ever entering the country again.

RABHA: And where would we do our shopping then?

[EVE *appears, crying, george patting her on the shoulder.*]

EVE: I'm finished, George.

GEORGE: No. Don't say that.

HIKMAT: What's wrong, George?

GEORGE: Poor girl, she's in love.

HIKMAT: But Fayez has been gone for a long time, why is she crying now?

GEORGE: It's not Fayez. Fayez was just one client!

ALL: Client?

GEORGE: Yes. It's David, the man who collects the money.

RABHA: Why are you crying? Has he abandoned you?

EVE: No. The doctor told me he's very sick and he's going to die.

KHUZAA: He deserves it. God might be patient, but He does not forget!

JASIR: This is the reward of sin. . . . What's wrong with him?

EVE [bursting into tears]: He's got Aids!

[A moment of stunned silence, then each starts wailing and slapping his own face.]

KHUZAA: You're doomed, Khuzaa!

JASIR: God, I beseech you to cure me!

LUQMAN: I repent. It's the last time, give me a chance . . .

SAKHR [whispering]: Did you do it?

ANTAR: I did, did you?

SAKHR: I did.

MUSTAFA [to HIKMAT]: It's all your fault! You wished me ill!

HIKMAT: God is my witness I never harbor any vindictive feelings! It's you, our men, you're like creepers, always stretching to reach further out.

RABHA [to KHUZAA]: Here's what you gain from your filthy national missions!

HIKMAT [to EVE]: Put our minds at rest. Did you have a test?

EVE: Yes, I've had all the necessary blood tests.

RABHA: And?

EVE: I'm not sick.

ALL: Thanks be to God.

GEORGE: Wait, she could still be a carrier.

EVE [*looking at them with hatred*]: That's true, and I could infect others.

ALL: You cheap whore!

GEORGE: Eve, go to your room.

EVE [*on her way out*]: I pray to God you all die and my lover lives! [*Exit.*]

HIKMAT: From now on, you all stay away from us . . . we have nothing to say to each other.

RABHA: What are we staying with them for right now? They're full of disease!

[*They exit.*]

GEORGE: Listen to me, you must all go for a test, immediately.

ALL: No, George.

MUSTAFA: Just the mention of this horrible disease gives us the creeps; it's depressing.

GEORGE [*amazed*]: And how are you going to know the truth?

SU'DUD: We don't wish to know the truth.

LAYTH: Because as long as we don't know, we have hope.

GEORGE: Hope without treatment, without medication?

ANTAR: What is with you? We can do what we please with our lives!

GEORGE: My dear, harm yourselves and nobody gives a damn! But you are not allowed to spread your diseases around! [*Exit GEORGE.*]

MUSTAFA: Brothers, we are all susceptible to error. It seems right for each of us to admit his mistakes and sins, and who knows . . . maybe God will forgive us and save us.

YAZID [*surprised*]: Mistakes and sins . . . like what?

MUSTAFA: You all understand me very well. Everyone who was at the brothel that night speak up!

ADHAM: By God you're right. But why don't we start with you?

MUSTAFA: I was there, just to get an idea. And God is my witness, I have not committed even half a sin! [*Brief silence.*] So? Nobody else?

JASIR: I went there to keep an eye on you.

SAKHR: I went to study Western behavior for my play.

ANTAR: I only went to stop the rest of you from going in!

LUQMAN: I was worried you might be taken advantage of. I thought you might need my help.

KHUZAA: I went to try it once then repent. Does this make me a sinner?

SAYF: I committed no fornication. As for feasting my eyes, that's no sin!

MUSTAFA: Briefly, it's clear that we all went to the brothel. The question is, why did we hide it from each other? Is it shame or fear of each other?

SAKHR: Are we really brothers?

ANTAR: Do we love each other?

SU'DUD: Or are we trapped with each other?

JASIR: It's because we despise our weaknesses; we vent our rage on each other.

KHUZAA: And because foreigners are way ahead of us, there's no point envying them. That's why we leave them and compete with each other.

TAMMAM: Does this mean we are the victims or the perpetrators?

ADHAM: I wonder, is God on our side or is He with the truth?

MIGHWAR: Is our unity the secret of our strength or our weakness?

LAYTH: And does the fact that we are brothers cancel the reality of our differences: Babylonians and Berbers, Phoenicians and Pharaohs?

MUSTAFA: Brothers, let's take an oath . . . even if we are to die tomorrow, we are still today's children!

ALL: Agreed.

MUSTAFA: The first thing we do is testify that Fayez was with us, to absolve him of the accusations of terrorism.

ADHAM: By God, this makes sense. . . . But are we to falsify our testimony?

SAKHR: Would you prefer to admit that we spent the night cavorting while he was struggling on his own? That would be unjust!

ANTAR: Brother, we are all brothers, so why should he be any different? I am sure he too was at the brothel.

MIGHWAR: And he was probably attacked there. Have you forgotten the robbers?

LAYTH: No, we all remember the details of their masks.

SU'DUD: Then we report them. And if the police fail to return Fayez, we avenge him ourselves.

[GEORGE *returns.*]

GEORGE: Are you still here? I've notified the hospital and they're coming to test you by force.

KHUZAA: No, George, have mercy!

[EVE *appears.*]

EVE: They don't need to have any tests, George. They're all ignorant and don't know that a simple kiss doesn't transmit the virus!

GEORGE [*laughing*]: A simple kiss? So everybody's in the clear! [*On his way out.*] A simple kiss! Hee hee hee!

[*Brief silence. all avert their eyes from each other.*]

MUSTAFA: Let's thank God that that's as far as it went. Now we must fulfill our vow.

ALL [*surprised*]: Vow? What vow?

MUSTAFA: Confess that we were at the brothel together.

LUQMAN: Wait. We didn't consider how this would make us look in front of our parents and people.

ANTAR: If I confess, my father will skin me alive.

SAKHR: It's better for me that I not go home.

SAYF: My family would deprive me of my inheritance.

MUSTAFA: We can't report the thieves unless we confess our mistake.

ADHAM: You want us to rescue Fayez by throwing ourselves into the deep end?

MIGHWAR: A dollop of discipline. We don't all have to confess. One of us can say he was at the brothel with Fayez.

JASIR: Mustafa . . . buddy, your parents are kind and tolerant. . . . That is, if you confess it won't be such a big deal!

MUSTAFA: What? So you all get to look pure and I'm the only degenerate in the whole group?

ANTAR: What is the matter, Mustafa . . . someone has to make a sacrifice, and you are the eldest . . .

MUSTAFA: Really? I'm the eldest in times of distress, but in good times we're all equal. Oh yes, I've heard that one before!

ADHAM: You have the morals of a knight!

MUSTAFA: That's between us. But in front of everybody else you make me look like a coward and you cry Shame! He frequents nightclubs! . . . Over my dead body, pal!

KHUZAA: How do we solve this problem?

MUSTAFA: First we have to recognize we have a problem.

TAMMAM: We *do* have a problem.

SAKHR: A baffling problem.

ANTAR: A chronic problem.

SAYF: Whenever we try to solve it . . .

KHUZAA: It gets more complicated.

SU'DUD: We ask left and right . . .

ADHAM: Nobody wants to guide us.

LUQMAN: Because we neither ask seriously . . .

MIGHWAR: Nor do we intend to listen.

HIKMAT: Behind every answer lie a million questions . . .

RABHA: Embarrassing questions . . . terrifying questions.

YAZID: Questions . . . questions . . .

LAYTH: And no answers.

JASIR: Questions demanding answers.

RABHA: Let's start over.

SU'DUD: We have a problem . . .

ALL: We can't solve.

LUQMAN: Because all possible solutions . . .

SAYF: Need hard work and effort.

KHUZAA: And actions need to be preceded by thought.

ADHAM: And thought to us . . .

MUSTAFA: Is a problem.

TAMMAM: We *do* have a problem.

SAKHR: A baffling problem.

ANTAR: A chronic problem.

ALL: With no solutions.

[*Action freezes.*]

The studio.

CAMERAMAN: I too went to the brothel. But here I am, I came out of it safe and sound, clean as a whistle.

F. ANNOUNCER: But even you, Lutfi, kept your mouth shut and wouldn't talk to the police.

CAMERAMAN: I had nothing for the robbers to steal.

M. ANNOUNCER: How did they all think of wearing a second mask, without prior agreement?

DIRECTOR: Because, in spite of their differences, they're all alike! It's you who refuse to believe in Arab unity!

M. ANNOUNCER [*surprised*]: And you, you still believe in it? We're all alike in one respect: we all deceive each other.

DIRECTOR: So what? One mustn't hang out one's dirty linen for all to see. If they hide the truth, it means they're embarrassed, unlike those shameless foreigners.

F. ANNOUNCER: Correct.

M. ANNOUNCER: Friends, the problem is not their spending the night at the brothel. That's not the end of the world. The problem is that, because they refuse to confess their mistakes, they are committing the greater sin.

F. ANNOUNCER: Correct.

DIRECTOR: Bear in mind that their confession would be detrimental to Fayez's case. They are his brethren.

F. ANNOUNCER: Correct.

M. ANNOUNCER: The truth can never be detrimental to a just cause.

F. ANNOUNCER: Correct.

DIRECTOR: The truth is not our business. Our business is to alter the image of the Arabs. Isn't this the aim of our program?

M. ANNOUNCER [*hesitantly*]: No. Actually, yes. But that's wrong, we are supposed to . . . to alter the reality itself . . . not the image.

DIRECTOR: How? Do we have any power or responsibility? Have you forgotten who you are?

F. ANNOUNCER: But I also understood differently.

DIRECTOR: The recommendations of the meeting of Arab ministers were clear from the beginning: "Endeavor to alter the image of the Arabs."

F. ANNOUNCER: That's why they told us to speak freely.

M. ANNOUNCER: But when we leave the reality unchanged and beautify the image, we are not educators . . . we'd be leading people astray . . . we'd be forgers of the truth.

DIRECTOR: No, mister. We would be patriots serving our nation by presenting the West with a good image of ourselves.

F. ANNOUNCER: Correct.

M. ANNOUNCER: Present the West with our image? The West is aware of all our secrets! They spy on us with satellites up above. They carry out thousands of scientific studies and experiments down below!

DIRECTOR: I have no time for these Byzantine discussions. I've received a contract for a job in an Arab country and I'll be leaving soon. If you'll excuse me. [*Exit.*]

F. ANNOUNCER: I was wrong. You are right, Mr. Amin.

M. ANNOUNCER: He's gone to add the final touches to the forged image we are using to fool the simple people who are watching us now!

CAMERAMAN: Nobody can fool us, pop! It goes in one ear and out the other!

F. ANNOUNCER: Correct, Mr. Lutfi. [*Hesitates.*] I no longer know where to find the truth.

CAMERAMAN: Forget academic gibberish. We're all right. By the life of our Prophet, we are as sweet as nectar, you just don't realize it. But if you insist on upsetting yourselves, do as you please. I'm not upsetting myself. [*Exit.*]

M. ANNOUNCER [*with emotion*]: Sadiqa . . .

F. ANNOUNCER [*distracted*]: The world's no longer beautiful.

M. ANNOUNCER: That's because we don't see its true face. Because the whole world is hiding behind a huge mask. [*As he turns around, she is gone. He holds a mask.*] One mask on top of another . . . that's the problem. Hypocrites have two faces, liars have four . . . but us, we have hundreds! The truth, to us, is a sacred duty, but it's lost. Whoever brings it to us deserves a prize . . . one hundred thousand whip lashes then the gallows. That's the problem.

Lights out.

SCENE VIII

The hotel. ALL *standing as frozen in last scene.* INSPECTOR *enters suddenly.*

INSPECTOR: Excuse me.

SOME: Inspector, sir!

INSPECTOR: I'm sorry to interrupt your pleasant conversation, but I'm obliged to inform you that you have been charged with disturbance of the public peace in Hyde Park today.

HIKMAT: But we were the victims!

RABHA: Yes, we are the victims.

INSPECTOR: In principle, I'm not in charge of investigating this trouble, but if it's related to Fayez's case . . .

SAKHR: If you want to prove Fayez's innocence, I want you to know that an unidentified caller contacted us one month ago and demanded a ransom of one hundred thousand dollars for his safe return. He said "Pay up or I'll kill him."

INSPECTOR: Did Fayez himself speak to you on the phone?

[ALL *exchange confused glances.*]

MUSTAFA: No. But the caller swore by his honor that he abducted him.

INSPECTOR: How can you be sure he wasn't tricking you?

SAKHR: And who would think of such a devilish deed?

INSPECTOR: It was you who made up a story about abduction; somebody else picked up on it and sold it back to you.

ALL [*astonished, confused, and disbelieving*]: No! Impossible!

HIKMAT: If Fayez hasn't been abducted, can you tell us why he's disappeared?

INSPECTOR: I ask the questions here. Lab tests have proved that the bookshop fire was perpetrated by a gang.

LAYTH: God is Great! Long live Arab unity!

INSPECTOR: And each of you has testified to being alone in his room on Saturday evening, so none of you has an alibi!

MUSTAFA: But we weren't suspects to begin with, your excellency.

INSPECTOR: Correct. But now you are. By the way, do these papers belong to you?

LAYTH: Yes, this is the brothers' handwriting.

INSPECTOR [*reading*]: "I swear, I will kill ten heathen foreigners. Ten dead will not quench my thirst, I will throw a bomb at them and burn them all . . . " Do you need any stronger evidence?

MUSTAFA: No, Inspector, sir, you're mistaken. This isn't for real, it's our rehearsal.

INSPECTOR: I know. A rehearsal for an armed attack!

SAKHR: No. This is a play, not real.

INSPECTOR [*smiling*]: And who, may I ask, plays the leading role?

[ALL *quiet, exchanging looks.*]

LAYTH: We all share the leading role, and we . . .

SAYF [*interrupting*]: Speak for yourself, brother!

INSPECTOR: Anyway, the 'play' excuse is amusing.

SAKHR: Believe us, it's not an excuse.

[AMAL *enters, shouting.*]

AMAL: Kill them, men! Slay them wherever you find them. Slay and show no mercy!

INSPECTOR: Is this the rest of the play?

LAYTH: No, these are her true feelings.

HIKMAT: We told you to shut up.

AMAL: Who saw Fayez today?

INSPECTOR: Do you know Fayez's whereabouts?

AMAL: His friends know where he is but they won't tell you.

RABHA: Don't believe her. It's all her grief over Fayez.

MUSTAFA: Spare her the questioning right now, Inspector, sir . . . you see how distraught she is!

LAYTH: Go rest in your room, Amal . . . rest.

AMAL: Brother Layth, the breeze of my heart and my soul . . . how many have you killed today?

LAYTH: I'm not playing this role . . . you mean Yazid!

YAZID: I'm not with you, I have no role. Look at me carefully, do I look like a man who would slay tens and scores?

INSPECTOR: My duty is limited to directing accusations. But your lawyer may answer in court.

ALL [*terrified*]: Court??

INSPECTOR: By the way, I advise you all that you may not leave the country without permission from the investigative authority concerned. Good evening! [*Tips his hat and leaves.*]

SAKHR: It all started with one of us missing; now we're all hostages!

KHUZAA: How I wish we *were* hostages! . . . We would have been asked for ransom and paid it!

SU'DUD: Let them abduct me, I haven't a penny! They might give *me* money!

AMAL [*with joy*]: You're all hostages? You have all become Fayez? . . . Oh joy! You are all mighty, brave men!

ADHAM: There goes our academic future down the drain!

MUSTAFA: Just our academic future? There go our freedom and our reputation!

JASIR: Had I stuck to my decision to leave your gang, I wouldn't have been entangled in your bloody mess!

[*The phone rings.* GEORGE *enters and answers.*]

SAKHR: What do we do now?

ANTAR: We must contact our parents immediately.

GEORGE: Phone for you.

ANTAR [*terrified*]: Daddy!!

MUSTAFA: He means for all of us . . . May God bring good news . . . [*On the phone.*] Allo? . . . Who's speaking?

AMAL [*in another world, starts singing a national anthem*]: My beloved homeland . . .

MUSTAFA: It's the attorney appointed by the Union of Arab Attorneys to defend Fayez's case.

ALL: We thank Thee, God!

MUSTAFA [*on the phone*]: You've come at the right time, sir. Yes, we've got news.

AMAL [*singing loudly*]: . . . *the mightiest nation* . . .

MUSTAFA [*raising his voice*]: No, no sign of Fayez . . . he didn't return. . . . We don't know . . .

ALL: Tell him to forget Fayez now!

MUSTAFA: Fayez's case is no longer the problem. We're talking about our own case. . . . We're all heading for disaster and you either catch us in time or you don't!

AMAL [*still singing the anthem*]: . . . *day after day, your glories increase* . . .

MUSTAFA: Who are we?? . . . We're all the Arab students . . . colleagues of Fayez.

KHUZAA: Dear God, let it be all right . . .

AMAL [*singing*]: . . . *its life is a bastion of victories . . . my homeland . . .*
Lights out.

EPILOGUE

F. ANNOUNCER: Dear viewers . . .

M. ANNOUNCER: Allow us . . .

F. ANNOUNCER: To sign off at the end of your program . . .

M. ANNOUNCER: Which is supposed to reach you . . .

F. ANNOUNCER: In all the Arab states.

M. ANNOUNCER: If you are watching us now . . .

F. ANNOUNCER: Our message must have reached you.

M. ANNOUNCER: Or rather, a segment of our message.

F. ANNOUNCER: For God only knows . . .

M. ANNOUNCER: How much remains . . . and how much has been censored.

F. ANNOUNCER: In closing, we can only . . .

M. ANNOUNCER: Leave you with our conclusion . . .

BOTH: Namely . . .
[BOTH *speak, but we cannot hear them. Someone has shut off the sound. Program signature tune.*]
Final curtain.